THE UNT.

CHILDREN'S FICTION

Na Willa and the House in the Alley, by Reda Gaudiamo, translated from Indonesian by Ikhda Ayuning Maharsi Degoul and Kate Wakeling, illustrated by Cecillia Hidayat

We Are A Circus, by Nasta, illustrated by Rosie Fencott

Oskar and the Things, by Andrus Kivirähk, illustrated by Anne Pikkov, translated from Estonian by Adam Cullen

CHILDREN'S POETRY COLLECTIONS

Eggenwise, by Andrea Davidson, illustrated by Amy Louise Evans

Balam and Lluvia's House, by Julio Serrano Echeverría, translated from Spanish by Lawrence Schimel, illustrated by Yolanda Mosquera

Cloud Soup, by Kate Wakeling, illustrated by Elīna Brasliņa

The Bee Is Not Afraid of Me: A Book of Insect Poems, edited by Fran Long and Isabel Galleymore, illustrated by Emma Dai'an Wright

SHORT STORIES AND ESSAYS

Parables, Fables, Nightmares, by Malachi McIntosh

How Kyoto Breaks Your Heart, by Florentyna Leow

Night-time Stories, edited by Yen-Yen-Lu

Tiny Moons: A year of eating in Shanghai, by Nina Mingya Powles

The Secret Box, by Daina Tabūna, tr. from Latvian by Jayde Wiil

POETRY COLLECTIONS

Europe, Love Me Back, by Rakhshan Rizwan

POETRY AND ART SQUARES

The Strange Egg, by Kirstie Millar, illustrated by Hannah Mumby

The Fox's Wedding, by Rebecca Hurst, illustrated by Reena Makwana

Pilgrim, by Lisabelle Tay, illustrated by Reena Makwana

One day at the Taiwan Land Bank Dinosaur Museum, written and illustrated by Elīna Eihmane

The Untameables

by Clare Pollard

illustrated by Reena Makwana

THE EMMA PRESS

To Gruff and Cate:
I wrote this for you

THE EMMA PRESS

First published in the UK in 2024 by The Emma Press Ltd.

Text © Clare Pollard 2024.
Cover design and interior artwork © Reena Makwana 2024.

ISBN 978-1-915628-26-8

A CIP catalogue record of this book
is available from the British Library.

Printed and bound in the UK by TJ Books, Padstow.
Typeset by Emma Dai'an Wright.

The Emma Press
theemmapress.com
hello@theemmapress.com
Birmingham, UK

Camelot

The Woods

Giant Country

Barking Beck

Tarquin's Tower

Castle of Maidens

Corbonek

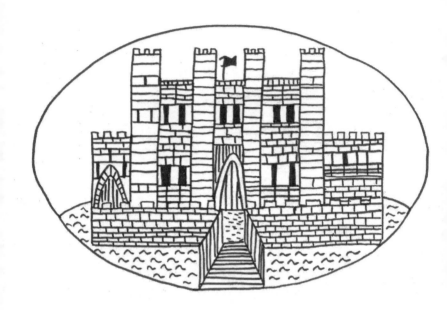

Welcome to Camelot, the home of King Arthur.

Yes, it's real.

I know it's hard to imagine, after so many years, so many losses, but it's important to try.

Come, let me show you. This is a land where there is still enchantment. Before the forest was razed; before the extinctions. The deep green woodland is lit by primroses and bluebells in the spring, and in autumn berries roll on the floor like spilt beads. Red deer munch, beavers build their dams and bears nap. At night howls make the canopy shiver.

Look at the dragon in its nest: its scales and sharp-boned wings. A baby eats a morsel of regurgitated mouse from its beak. You think it impossible, but when they existed they were no more impossible than the lynx or grass snake – they were everyday creatures.

A boggart giggles as she curdles milk; a griffin care-fully scrapes a burrow into the cliff with her paws and squats on it to lay eggs. A faerie in a gossamer dress trips over a toadstool. A green-skinned giant pulls on his muddy boots.

And look, in the heart of all this wonder and wild-ness, at the castle of Camelot: its pale, tall walls cut with narrow slits for arrows. Its deep moat and draw-bridge and many guards; its defences of catapults and cauldrons of boiling oil. Inside are men who hate this land, and will in time destroy it – who only trust what they can conquer, rule or own.

They sit in the Great Hall around a round table, and every chair says something on it like 'Strongest Knight' or 'World's Best Knight' or 'Cleverest Knight' in glowing golden letters, and they eat meat, drink wine out of jewelled goblets and bray about what heroes they are. 'Here's to another dead traitor!' they like to toast, about whoever didn't agree with them that week.

Perhaps you're thinking: Hang on, I thought those knights of the round table were nice guys! You think you've heard stories like this before, but the truth is you haven't.

Sir Lionel has just defeated the Black Knight, for example, and in the usual tale he's portrayed as a lordly defender of Britain – so famous for defeating a fear-some and gigantic wild boar that ballads have been sung about him through the ages. In such versions his armour gleams; his sword has magical powers. He returns from fighting on his trusty milk-white steed, with the fair maiden he has rescued and will marry. She swoons in the saddle behind him, probably wear-ing pink. Everyone cheers.

But history is written by the powerful, who can never resist tweaking it a bit.

In actual fact, Sir Lionel is a blonde-haired thug who is always boasting that he once killed what was, in truth, just a constipated pig.

He returns to the castle gate in drizzle, with his horse Valiant badly wounded – limping and neighing pitifully. The bearded groom, John, greets him. 'Was the princess you went to rescue not there, sire?' he asks, seeing the saddle behind Sir Lionel is empty.

'Princess, ha! Some princess,' Sir Lionel snaps, still smarting from her escape. Not so keen on being 'rescued' after all, the princess pretended to need a wee behind a bush then, when at a good distance, stripped to her vest and knickers and dived into the river. It turned out she could swim a very brisk front-crawl.

'No helping some of these pagan plague-sores,' Lionel spits. 'She was making out she *liked* the Black Knight! I hurt her friend, apparently! Well boo hoo! She could have come to the court of Arthur, the Rightful King of Britain, with *me*, Sir Lionel, slayer of the fiercest hog that ever rolled in English mud and a knight of the round table! Thank you would have been the correct response, but *oh no…*'

Sir Lionel dismounts, the spurs on his heel smashing into Valiant's wounded side and making her whinny. 'Valiant's badly hurt,' John says. 'Did she fight the Black Knight courageously?'

'Courageous, that's a joke! Valiant! More like Vali-*isn't*' Sir Lionel says. 'This stupid old nag wouldn't even gallop after the princess after I gave her a stern whipping. Chop her into steaks and feed her to the hawks and hounds.'

'Oh I don't know if I need to…' John begins, nervously, but Sir Lionel grasps John by the neck with his big ham-coloured fist and pins him to the castle wall.

'*Audi, vide, tace,*' Sir Lionel spits, which means 'hear, see, be silent' in Latin. It's posh for 'shut up.' John doesn't understand of course, but Sir Lionel particularly loves speaking Latin when the other person doesn't understand it.

Luckily, it so happens that a ten-year old boy called Roan is passing at this moment with some of Sir Lionel's skinny greyhounds: Troy, Nameless, Amiable and Nosewise.

Roan, the dog boy, is to be the real hero of this story, although he would not enjoy me saying so because he does not like heroes. It seems to him that 'hero' is usually just another name for 'murderer'. The dad he can't remember died in one of Arthur's battles. Roan won't play sword-games, even though those are the only games the other boys play. If he sees someone or something hurting, the pain flinches through him too.

'Kill the horse, now,' Sir Lionel orders John, scowling with bloodthirst, holding out his sword. 'Go on, I don't tolerate rebellion. Let me see you butcher it.'

Roan has dark hair, long lashes, his mother's full lips. He is tanned from always being outside, thin and gentle, with a little perpetual cough. Panic floods through Roan at what he's just heard. He looks at Valiant's gentle, bowed head. How breath pours through her nostrils, hot and sad.

Her watery eyes seem to plead with him to do something.

Okay, Roan thinks, shaking with adrenalin. *I'll do something.*

Roan is not actually very brave though.

In fact, if you want to know how scared Roan is of knights on a scale of one to ten, it is three million six hundred thousand and ninety-six.

But John is taking the sword, his hand trembling. Roan has to act *now*. It is then that he has an idea. A great idea! A very – oh. Oh no. It is a very brave idea, which is the last thing Roan wants.

Still, Valiant's moist eyes continue to look at him hopefully. Gulping back his fear, he whispers to the greyhounds: *'Pups. I have a plan. I need you to welcome your master Sir Lionel back. Yes, I know we don't like him, but this is important. For me. Your BIGGEST welcome, alright?'* The dogs seem to nod, and...

RUFF, WOOF, BOW-WOW-WOW!

It works! When Roan slips them off their leashes, the greyhounds go crazy! They race towards Sir Lionel all at once, leaping up and knocking him to the floor with a clanging of armour, CLUNK, CLANK, and pounce on his chest and lick his face through the helmet with their shiny doggy tongues. 'Bleugh!' Sir Lionel shouts, which is not Latin. 'TONGUES! Slimy, bone-stinking, slop-mouthed TONGUES, in my eyes! I need a wipe, CAN'T SEE...'

'So sorry, sire,' Roan apologises. 'You know how much they love their master. Please be merciful. Come on, dogs!' he adds, rather half-heartedly, whilst he watches John slipping away with Valiant out of the corner of his eye. 'Get off him now.'

Eventually he pulls the dogs off. Sir Lionel gets up from the puddle of drool, slipping with fury.

'If that happens again,' he barks at Roan, blinking away gloop, 'you'll be sacked, you little hedge-born churl. We'll kick you out of Camelot and you'll never see your family again. Let's see how you fare out *there*, in the wild, with the monsters and wolves!'

'Yes sire, sorry sire, I'll make sure they don't do it again,' Roan stammers, bowing as low as he can, because he still thinks he's lucky to live in Camelot. Everyone knows that the court of Arthur, the Rightful King of Britain, is the greatest place in the world!

Isn't it?

II

That evening, in the leaky hayloft behind the castle brewery, Roan hugs Valiant, fingers catching in her blood-crusted silver mane. 'O Valiant, you poor thing,' Roan says, his chin crumpling. She's the horse John sometimes lets him ride, who likes to nuzzle treats out of his palm. 'O Valiant, I'm so sorry you're hurt.'

'She'll be right,' John says, warmly. 'She'll heal, don't worry, same as the others.' This is where they hide creatures who can't be tamed: those who have angered the nobles or knights and must be kept away from view. See that beagle curling on the hay? It once bit King Arthur's nose. That other horse, Goldentrot, launched Guinevere into a bog. Vesper the peregrine falcon kept going for the trainer's eyeballs with her beak, whilst that dappled goat called Pocket, which currently seems to be eating a bucket, once munched a hole in Sir Lancelot's best pyjamas in a place where you definitely wouldn't want a hole.

'You're too soft,' John tells Roan. 'You need to man up a bit, stop feeling everything so much. Toughen up. I can teach you to fight if you want to know a few moves. I see those other boys bullying you, you know.' But Roan shakes his head.

'Thanks for this afternoon, anyway,' John says. 'You sure know how to talk to the animals, you do. Go on, lad. Remember to check both ways before you leave here – don't want anyone spotting you. Now go and see your mum.'

'Put some honey on Valiant's wound,' Roan says, anxious about leaving his favourite horse. 'That's good for cuts, isn't it?'

'Honey! The kitchen'll smell her and roast her up for a feast.'

'The cut needs dressing, John. Please?'

'Okay,' John says. 'I'll find summat.'

Roan heads for his mum and sister's room. He likes its homely, body smell; the warm glow of the tallow candle.

His little sister Gwen, three, has a wild massive tangle of pale hair, always hopping with lice, and when he gets there their mother, Bonnie, is trying to comb it. The knots are so bad they must be elf-locks, which the little folk tangle in the hair of sleeping children. Bonnie plucks out a nit with her fingers. '… So that's why you shouldn't be rude to the knights,' she's saying.

'You'll get in trouble, my darling.'

'They stink,' Gwen says, her lower lip jutting out with disgust. She has the most expressive face ever. 'They stink like parps.' And then her eyes go round and she starts to giggle, hee-hee. 'I just parped, Muma. Sorr-ee.'

'That's disgusting,' Roan says, which it is, although he can't help smiling at her. 'That's worse than the kennels.'

'I am your cute little stinky puppy, Roan,' Gwen tells him, sticking out her tongue and panting like a dog. 'Woof woof.'

'Hey Roan,' his mum says. 'Gwen needs to listen to me this time. Can you talk some sense into her? I'm serious. I'm worried. She actually shouted 'Knights are YUKKY' at Sir Bors today.'

'He was picking his nose,' Gwen giggles.

'He's a knight,' Bonnie says. 'He's *more important* than you. Don't you understand? You don't get to tell him off. You're going to get punished, or—' her voice breaks off in desperation. She is twenty-something, but somehow old already: grey streaks in her brown curls, raw hands. She has felt terrible all month: weak and feverish, like she is coming down with something.

'Listen to Mum, Gwen,' Roan says, uselessly, as his sister has already started crossing her eyes to make him laugh. It's true, though. They're going to have to hide Gwen in the stable with the other untameables soon, if she carries on this way.

'Bor-ring,' Gwen says. Roan notices she is feeding a mouse in her pocket with a bit of crust. 'Her name is Binka,' Gwen tells him. 'I just made that name up.'

'She's cute.'

'She bites,' his mum warns him. 'Are you alright, Roan love? You seem down.'

'Oh, a horse got wounded again,' he says. 'Valiant. I hope she'll get better.'

'You love your animals, don't you? Kind boy.'

'How about you, are you alright?' he asks his mum.

'Oh, just a bug, I'm sure it's nothing. I'd better not hug you, though.'

'I'll do it,' Gwen tells Roan, brightly, and she gives him her most squeezy hug. Roan hugs her back – he likes hugs – and the mouse runs up his shirt, which tickles.

Afterwards Roan goes to the kennel. Part of his job is sleeping with the hunting dogs, to keep them from fighting. It's considered a good job, because the kennel is actually heated and he can sleep with the dogs on oak beds, which is better than most servants get. But it's hard to sleep tonight, Roan finds he's worrying again: about Valiant, his mum, his sister. Troy licks his hand and he can smell the blood on her teeth.

He realises that Camelot always smells of blood.

III

Morning begins in the dark, under the spittle of stars. You can see your breath. In the kennel, Roan pulls his tunic over his head and begins his to-do list: feed the hounds, get fresh water for their bowls, change their straw. They must be pampered and fussed over. They leap joyfully around his legs. 'Morning, Clench,' he says. 'Morning, Brag, ooh, that's some real dog-breath you have today. Cabal, how's your tummy? Would some grass settle it? Is that a thorn in your paw, Nameless? Ooch, let's get that out.'

When his chores are done, some of the knights take their dogs. Sir Lionel is going on a hunting jaunt with his brother, Sir Bors. Sir Lionel, his floppy golden fringe bobbing over his massive jaw, is still angry with Roan for the licking and has decided there is a single flea in Troy's water bowl, although Roan can't see anything. 'He'll be sick, you dumb little lubber-wart. *Fresh* water, from the spring.'

'It was fresh, sire,' Roan stutters, trying not to cry. He can't help it – when he's told off he always feels his chin wobbling.

'Don't you dare speak back!' Sir Lionel fumes. 'The nerve of you! You're the dog boy, you mangy little mongrel, and you know what? You can't even control them, as you proved yesterday. I should – ugh.' He kicks Roan, hard, on the knees, then – *oof* – in the stomach, then smooths his fringe back down and laughs. He begins to sound his horn. Roan tries to blink his tears away before they see the glint. These men think crying is pathetic.

'Look at my new spear,' Sir Bors grunts at Roan, tapping it menacingly on his chest. 'Sharp.' Sir Bors is always red, like a thumb that has been trapped in a door.

They gallop away with the hounds.

Once the dogs are gone Roan has time to eat his breakfast: a chunk of bread, still coarse with the grit from the grinding stones. He thinks he'll check on his mum, but unfortunately runs into the other castle boys who are play-fighting in the courtyard again. 'Die like herring, you filthy mermaids!' Acwel is shouting. 'I'll shoot you with my bow and arrow, twang, whheeee, thunk, uurrrrgh...'

Acwel and Pierce love attacking each other and invisible enemies and also anything real that gets in their way. Roan tries to sneak past them, but they knock him to the ground and put a pointy stick to his throat. 'Beg for mercy, you traitor,' Pierce says. 'I'll chop your head off and stick it on a spike!' He likes sticking heads on spikes. Sometimes Pierce impales frogs or elves on spikes and watches them die.

'Let's chop his winkle off!' Acwel shouts gleefully. He's obsessed with winkles.

'If he even has one.'

'Let's open his guts up and feed his innards to his dogs.'

The stick makes it hard to breathe. 'Mercy,' Roan coughs, as a foot pushes his mouth towards the dirt. 'Mercy, mercy.' They let him go.

'You going to cry now, Roan?' Pierce asks. 'Go and cry to your useless scrubber of a mum.'

Roan swallows, bows his head and walks on. Ashamed because they're right: he is going to see his mum. He'll probably cry again, too.

His mother is lying on her bed, her face clenched into a wince. Roan is very worried about her now. He doesn't think she's eaten for two days. 'I hope you didn't work this morning,' he says.

'I had to clean the Great Hall first thing,' she says. 'But then I passed out, so they carried me back! It's my chest that hurts – it feels like there's a knot in there.'

Roan feels panicked. A couple of people in the castle have found such lumps recently, and some of them have died. Everyone is saying there's something wrong with the water. Her face is shining with sweat.

'Me and Binka gave her breakfast,' Gwen says, stroking her mum's forehead. 'There, there.'

He chats to them for a bit, and then hears the horns – the knights are returning. Roan steps out to sees them arrive, dragging corpses. As the shapes come nearer, he can see it is a deer and a unicorn, its white side stained with red. Roan can feel that sour flavour rising in his throat.

The knights also have a goblin mewling in a cage. They are suspicious of magic folk, quick to arrest them for betrayal. This is another for the dungeon, where there are walls of chained-up werefoxes and trolls; faeries with their wings rotting away.

The hounds run to Roan and jump up happily to see him, licking his hands. 'Hey, dog boy,' says Sir Lionel, dismounting. 'Sort these hounds out.'

It is at that very moment that Binka the mouse scurries in front of them. A tiny, furry, zig-zagging blink of trouble. Sir Bors – angry he's made the least kills today – is quick and determined. With a furious, twisted glare he leaps to attention, raises his spear and thrusts rapidly at the mouse.

'Very sharp,' Bors grins pinkly, holding up Binka's little corpse skewered like a kebab.

Gwen runs outside to find her mouse and crashes straight into Sir Lancelot.

'Sorry,' Roan splutters in panic, fear rushing through him. 'I'm sorry, my sister didn't mean to—'

But it is too late. Gwen sees Binka's skewered

and starts screaming. Not screaming in horror, ~~ugh~~ – screaming in pure rage at Sir Bors. 'BINKA BINKA BINKA! YOU KILLED MY BEST PET!!! NOOOOO!!! You are a YUKKY knight and I hate you and YOU ARE POOPY AND YUK!'

Sir Bors pushes her over with his shield. 'SHALL I SPEAR YOU TOO?' he demands, turning a purplish crimson. 'WHO IS THIS LITTLE WITCH?'

'I AM GWEN!!!!' Gwen screams from within her massive nest of hair, shaking her little fists and kicking her feet. 'I WANT MY BINKA!!'

'I'm sorry, I'm sorry, mercy, mercy,' Roan begs, trying to scoop her up, putting his hand over her mouth like his mother does. She bites him, livid now. 'She's three, she's just three.' He's thinking Bors will kill her like a mouse.

'I'M BIG THREE,' Gwen shouts through his fingers, and she roars like a lion: 'RAAAARRRRR!'

And then Sir Lionel laughs. It is a cold laugh, but it calls for calm at least. It is a laugh that says he will not waste any more attention on her.

'Come on,' he says to the other knights. 'I need some booze after catching that unicorn.'

'I finished that mouse off, though,' Bors grunts. 'Did you see me? I stabbed it. Boom!'

'You did, brother,' Sir Lionel agrees. 'You did indeed do some excellent stabbing. Disappointed there were no boars today though. Remember when I wrestled that fearsome and gigantic wild boar? Did you know they've written a ballad about me now?' He bursts into slurring song. *'Sir Lionel at that boar sped / And sliced that massive hairy head.* Good tune, isn't it? Catchy? Of course, Mother always said I was destined for fame!'

They leave Roan with the dead things and his tantruming sister.

'Please,' he mutters to her. 'Please stop it, please.'

Why hasn't she learnt yet how dangerous Camelot is?

V

Now let me introduce you to a child who knows exactly how dangerous Camelot is.

Elva – who has reddish hair, freckles, and a brilliant brain – uses crutches because her spine is bent, something that makes one of her legs slightly longer than the other and her shoulder protrude forward when she walks, with difficulty. After she was born and they realised she wasn't growing normally, many superstitious people told her parents that Elva was a changeling. That their real baby had been stolen and Elva left in her place. That she was a faerie child: sickly, weird, ravenous. They said Elva's mum should test her by putting her in the fire, or whipping her, or making her eat foxgloves. They said she should be left out on the crags. Oh, all sorts of lovely ideas! So Elva is very wary of Camelot, and always careful not to draw too much attention to herself.

Elva's mother works in the kitchen whilst her dad waits on the table, so she's sometimes allowed to help peel turnips. It's not exactly a laugh a minute. Elva listens, though, as the wet peel unspools. Or she lies in the corridor outside the Great Hall, if she needs to lie down, which she does sometimes, waiting for her dad, and takes it all in. Elva has very good hearing. She might keep her mouth shut, mainly, but she hears everything tonight.

The knights eat everything. Or any meat, at least: what they enjoy is things that were alive and have been killed to fill their bellies. Wolf, eel, cat, a roasted swan served with a sauce of innards, ginger and its own blood. Boar's head is a favourite too, as the kitchen does a special trick that means it breathes fire. Once the head cook baked four and twenty blackbirds into a pie that sang when you cut it open, but one pooped on Lancelot's head so that didn't go down so well.

Tonight there is a sixteen-bird roast, which is a warbler inside a bunting inside a lark inside a thrush inside a quail inside a lapwing inside a plover inside a partridge inside a woodcock inside a teal inside a guinea fowl inside a duck inside a chicken inside a pheasant inside a goose inside a giant bustard.

The knights of the round table are very merry after the unicorn-killing. Its head will join the other trophies stuffed and mounted on the walls of the Great Hall. Sir Lionel, sitting in the seat that says 'Lordliest Knight', is the most roaringly drunk of course, and has just broken his second plate and pulled a serving boy's trousers down, shouting 'Errare humanum est!' (Which means 'to err is human' in posh twit.) Bors, in the 'Most Violent Knight' seat, is trying to eat a hedgehog with just his knife and it keeps stabbing him back.

Sir Lancelot, the 'Handsomest Knight', is mooning over Arthur's wife Guinevere, a bored beauty with whom he thinks he is in love although he has never actually spoken to her. He assumes she is passionately in love with him too. Occasionally she glances at him then whispers something behind her hand to a princess, which he guesses is 'I can't bear to live without that dishy hunk' but is actually more along the lines of 'Why is that sleazy saddle-goose goggling at me?'

Lancelot is a bit of an idiot. He thinks he is a talented romantic poet, although his lyrics contain rhymes like:

> *Your eyes are wise*
> *like owls that go hoot.*
> *Your lips are roses*
> *and your nose is a sweet musical flute.*

Now it's the fish course, but that's not quite what you might imagine. They call anything aquatic 'fish', so the choice tonight is between puffin, otter or porpoise porridge. 'Puffins,' Merlin smiles. 'Marvellous. Such delectable hearts.' Merlin's eyes always seem slightly distant, as though he is not in the room but plotting his next move. He has a bland, childish face but wants to look wise, so is experimenting with a long silver beard and a wholly unconvincing pointy hat.

'Yum goes my tum,' King Arthur says, picking meat off the little bones. His skull shines in the centre of his crown. Arthur is a basic and greedy man who always wants more of everything: more gold, more jewels, more power, more maidens, more pratfalling jesters, more land, more glory, more meat, more hair, higher body-counts, higher turrets.

King Arthur's armies have been away for a long time, fighting the traitorous Saxons, Scots and Picts to create his dream of a united kingdom that bows before him. But recently such shifting lines on a map seem underwhelming. Alright, so 960 Saxons were slaughtered the other week at Badon Hill, but what does that mean to him? He is feeling unsatisfied again; bored with the company of his knights, these relatives and sycophants.

King Arthur decides to stir it up. 'Christmas is coming,' he says. 'You know, there's a gift I'd like. But I expect none of you could get it for me. I mean, probably only the best knight in the world could get it for me.'

'What could such a gift be, sire?' Merlin asks, raising an eyebrow.

'The Holy Grail, Merlin,' Arthur says. 'Why, I overheard you talking about it to one of the squires just this morning. How it is the most super-powered, amazing, great, beautiful cup in the whole world and only the very best people are allowed near it.'

'Oh, did I say that?' Merlin says, unable to suppress that little smirk that flashes over his face when a plan is going well.

'What does it do, Merlin?' Sir Lionel asks. 'This cup?'

'It can heal,' Merlin says. Everyone's interest vanishes.

'Is that all?' Arthur says, suddenly looking disinterested. 'Never mind, then. I thought the trinket sounded more fun than that.'

'Healing's for girls,' Bors grunts.

'Don't criticise girls, Bors,' Lancelot says. 'No lady will be slandered on Lancelot's watch – I am a lady-lover.' He winks at Guinevere as he says this, making her do a little sick in her mouth.

'These knights are fools, sire,' Merlin says, thinking fast – for some reason he really wants this cup. 'Anyone who heal can be all-powerful. What use would your armies be if the soldiers they wounded could just stand up again good as new? Not to mention immortality. Such a grail would make you a god, basically. I've been worrying lately, your Majesty, knowing it's out there. Our power will never be absolute without it.'

'Mmm,' King Arthur says. 'My power's at an all-time high. We're doing great stuff, Merlin! I'm the best king of all time, people are saying.'

'Of course, but I mean everyone wants it,' Merlin

continues, laying it on rather thickly. 'It's the most sought-after object in the world. I've heard it has HUGE diamonds too and it says WINNER on it, because whoever wins it has basically won at life.'

'Winner, you say?' Arthur nods, sucking a rainbow beak clean. 'I see, yes. WINNER. Well, that does sound like a beautiful cup after all. The thing is, though, I also heard it could only be won by The Purest Most Righteous Brilliant Knight Ever.'

Everyone gasps, because there is an empty chair at the end of the table called The Perilous Seat. It says on the back, in glowing gold letters, 'The Purest Most Righteous Brilliant Greatest Knight Ever'. It also says, in the small print, 'if you are not and you sit on me you will die'.

No one has sat on it.

'I will try the quest,' a voice pipes up. Everyone looks at Sir Galahad, who has been eating so quietly in his seat – which says 'Youngest Knight' – that they have hardly noticed he is there. He has slick hair, a stiff posture, a pompous voice and, currently, his hand raised. 'I feel I am the purest amongst us, sire. I will fetch the grail and prove myself worthy of The Perilous Seat.'

'I will join you, then,' Sir Lionel says. 'It sounds like there's a ballad in this adventure!' He necks his goblet of mead and throws it over his shoulder.

'And me,' Bors yaps. 'We'll need to kill. Lots of killing.'

'And, oh, me too, of course, I suppose,' Sir Lancelot says, gazing on Guinevere again. 'A noble heart will submit to any test to prove its, erm, valour.'

'That's settled, then,' Arthur says. 'Castle Carbonek is where you head. My old rival King Pelles' home – apparently he's wounded and it's a total wasteland round there, very unlike our marvellous Camelot! Anyway, it's something to do with this cup and I want to make sure we get it, not him. Christmas is coming early, eh! Here's to the quest for the Holy Grail!'

'To the quest for the Holy Grail,' the knights toast, as Elva's father brings in the unicorn on a silver platter, marinated in cloves and roasted on the griddle.

And, lying in the shadows of the corridor, Elva – who has heard everything – has an idea.

VI

The next week Bonnie's chest has darkened and turned scaly, like a dragon's wing. Roan begins to feel shaky with terror. One morning he goes beyond the castle walls to the edge of the wood just to get some space. A bog-caked unicorn drinks from the river, its horn translucent like an icicle. He leans over and splashes his face with icy water. *Breathe, Roan, come on.* But then he remembers what they are saying about the water and shuts his lips. Is it poisoning them all? He won't think of the word *dying*. He's not going to. She's not. She can't.

'She's dying, isn't she?' Elva says. She is lying on her back in a puddle of brown and red leaves, resting her back. He hadn't seen her there, in her brown dress with her red hair and freckles. He thinks of patterned adders lying in wait in the trees' dapple. 'Everyone's getting ill.'

'You can speak?' Roan says, quietly.

'Of course I can speak,' she says, sharply. 'My body's twisted, not my intellect, thanks.'

'But, I mean, you don't speak,' Roan mumbles. 'I've never heard you speak before.'

'You know how everyone says I'm a changeling?'

'Yes,' he admits. The other castle children call her broken and weird.

'Well, changelings are supposed to possess uncanny insight.'

'Oh.'

'And I do,' Elva says, looking at him super-intensely with her eyes, which he notices are green as ferns. 'So it's safest to keep my mouth shut. Mum and Dad tell me every day: Keep your mouth shut, Elva, and don't get us into trouble! You're already a burden on the community, don't remind them that you exist!'

'That's not very nice,' Roan says, feeling bad he's never paid much notice to her before.

'I'm glad you've come. I've been thinking all week I should tell you about the cure,' Elva informs him. 'There's the Holy Grail, a magic cup, and they say it can heal anyone. Merlin seems to really want it. The knights are all going on a quest to look for it next week.'

'What's that to do with me?' Roan asks.

'I hate Merlin, that wicked old trickster. He's all puffs of smoke, isn't he? Always telling everyone the pagans are enemies and King Arthur is destined to drive them out of Britain! Oh, is he really? Isn't that convenient!'

'You don't believe it's his destiny?' Roan asks, shocked by her words. He's never heard anyone else talk like this.

'Arthur's men murder thousands of Picts, Irish, Scots, giants, Saxons and gnomes! These islands are awash with blood because he claims he's the rightful king of Britain!' Elva declares, warming to her theme. 'But it's not Arthur's fault. Oh no. I mean, he's only fulfilling the prophecy. Didn't you read that stone with a sword in it? You know, the one Merlin just happened to stumble upon completely randomly in that yard?'

'You think *he* put the sword in the stone there?' Roan asks, utterly confused.

'Uh-huh.'

'You don't think the prophecy is true?'

'Total propaganda,' Elva hisses. She gestures at her freckles. 'My mum's half Pict. They're not 'savages', by the way.'

'But aren't they traitors?'

'They're just people like you and me, Roan,' Elva says.

Roan thinks. Can that be right? But now she says it, it sounds right. They do just look like people.

'I actually think Merlin's main problem is women,' Elva continues. 'He never shuts up about Vivien and Morgan le Fay trying to ruin Camelot, even though he's basically just a rubbish boy-witch. You know, I used to sneak into Merlin's library and read his spell-books: a boggart's toe, the wool of a bat, an ogre's tooth… They're just shopping-lists of death.' Words are flowing out of Elva now so quickly that Roan can hardly keep up. She looks pleased, like she thinks this is going well.

'You can read?' Roan asks. He can't, and he didn't think it was allowed, actually. Certainly not for girls. Not if you aren't noble.

'I told you, uncanny insight. The point is, the Holy Grail is meant to heal people. It would help your mum.'

'How, though?' Roan asks. 'Even if they found it and brought it back to Camelot, they wouldn't let us near it. They'd just lock it away with all their other treasure. The knights wouldn't let my mum's lips touch their precious grail, would they? They'd be scared a housemaid would soil it.' He's surprised how angry he sounds when he says that. It's dangerous to let yourself get angry. Aren't you meant to accept your place?

'That's not a problem,' Elva says. 'Because we're going to get it first.' Roan laughs.

'We are?'

'Yes.'

'Dog boy and the lame changeling?'

'Why not?'

'I would like to see the world outside Camelot,' he admits, shyly. 'I mean – I'd like to see the sea.'

'I'd like to solve a riddle,' Elva says. 'Or rescue someone. Have a real adventure, like in the books.'

'I'd like to see a real dragon,' Roan says. 'Not a head in a bag dragged back by a knight, but a real live one breathing flames from its nose. And a griffin. They've hunted all the ones near the castle – they say you can only find them now in the real wildwood.' He finds himself peering into the leafy depths beyond them.

'Let's go to the wildwood then.'

'Yeah, right.'

'No, Roan, really: I mean it.' Elva's fern-coloured eyes are shining like hope. He finds his heart is fluttering like a trapped bird.

'You can't,' he says. 'You can't walk well enough. What if we had to run?'

'We'll take some horses. You're good with horses.'

'I can't leave my mum.'

'Maybe you have to leave her to save her, Roan.'

'Why me?'

'You're the only boy in this castle who isn't horrible,' she says. 'I've been watching.' Roan swallows.

'Then you stay and look after her and Gwen, and I'll go. It'll be easier to follow them secretly on my own.'

'No,' Elva says, fiercely. 'Don't you steal my idea!'

'I'm thinking of you,' Roan says. 'What if there's fighting? You're a girl, you're—' He gestures at her body.

'Don't you patronise me,' Elva says. 'I'm coming

and that's it. Because I need this grail too, alright? Maybe I need to be healed as well, did you maybe think of that? They hate everyone different here! I won't spend my whole life playing the weird, mute girl everyone ignores or pities or thinks is creepy. Because that's not who I am. I'm not a turnip-peeler. Do you understand, Roan? That isn't me, okay? *That isn't me.* I don't want this so-called life they say I have to live.' She's almost hissing. Her pain flinches through him. Roan starts to cry, tears catching on his dark lashes.

'Sorry,' he says. 'Of course you're right, you should come.'

'I'm going to help you,' she says. 'You need my brains. Your sister can look after your mum while we're gone.'

'Gwen?! She's three!'

'Big three,' Elva says, and there's a smile in her voice that Roan can't resist. He looks at her and smiles back.

'Okay. I mean, sorry,' he wipes his nose on his fist. 'Sorry, I'm always crying.'

'I like it,' Elva says, looking back up at the slow rain of crimson leaves. 'It means you feel things.'

VII

A blue, damp dark. Roan wakes before everyone else, carefully lifting Cabal's tail off his leg. He can't quite believe he's doing this. He'd always assumed every day of his life would be the same, except people would grow up or grow ill, but this is so different it's like he's in a dream. He lights the fire as quietly as he can, fills the dog bowls, then tiptoes out. The stone floors sizzle with the rain. The first songs of blackbirds tinkle through the trees.

Roan goes to Bonnie and Gwen's bed. Bonnie is curled on her side, breathing heavily. Roan gives her the lightest kiss on the forehead, then he shakes his sister awake. Her eyes go round and she is about to shout something when he puts a finger over his lips and signals for her to come outside. Amazingly, she does. 'I do NOT want to wake, I want to sleep,' she snarls once outside, her lips pouting. 'You are yukky.'

'This is important,' Roan whispers. 'I'm going away for a couple of days to, erm. To get herbs to make Mum better. You have to look after her. She's not well. You have to be really kind to her, alright? Promise?'

'Muma,' Gwen says, her face crumpling into wilfulness. Her nightgown is up around her bum.

31

She shivers then gives her hair a good scratch. 'I want my MUMA NOW!'

'SSShhh, no, naughty,' he says, trying to sound firm. 'You're not to wake her if she's sleeping. She needs her sleep, do you understand? Please. That's naughty. Be my good Gwen.'

'I am NOT being naughty,' she says.

'Erm, good, good then. I love you, little sister,' he says, and he hugs her very tightly, and presses a final kiss into her lemon mane. 'Look after Mum and don't get yourself in trouble, okay? Keep your mouth shut. Promise?'

'Pinky promise.'

After this Roan heads to the hay loft where they keep the untameable animals. Elva is there, with one saddlebag that contains bread and cheese she has lifted from the kitchen, and another with a blanket, a beaker and some useful bits. It had also contained a knife, but she is in the middle of trying to wrestle that out of Pocket the goat's mouth before it's digested. 'I've got cloaks and helmets too,' she says. 'The suits of armour are too big, but these helmets will cover our faces, and it's still dark. When we get to the gate we just have to make sure it's open and then gallop out quickly like we own the place. Got it!'

Pop! She stumbles backwards, holding the goat-gnawed knife aloft in victory.

They are taking Valiant and Goldentrot, as no one will miss them except John the groom. Valiant's coat still has tender-looking scars on it. Roan will have to be careful not to kick her.

'They'll never let us come home again,' Roan says, suddenly scared.

'Don't be silly,' Elva says. 'The knights never notice us. We're all the same to them. They won't notice we've gone any more than they noticed these horses weren't in the stable anymore when you hid them.'

As they ride towards the gate it starts to rain. It bangs so hard on Roan's helmet it sounds like the apocalypse and he can barely see anything through the narrow eyeholes. It is so disorientating, he feels panic tightening his lungs. He is sure they are going to be caught. He is such an idiot.

But Elva's plan works like a dream. The guard is sheltering and just shouts 'Good morning sires' out of his hiding hole.

'Audentes fortuna iuvat,' Elva shouts back, in her most bellowing voice, as they ride on into the woods.

'What did that mean?' Roan asks, breathlessly. 'Was it a spell?'

'It's called Latin, I think,' Elva says. 'The Roman language. I'm not actually sure what it means, but it sounds very impressive, doesn't it?'

After a while they feel safe enough to remove their helmets. It's a Sunday. Elva says there's no way the knights would set off on a quest on Sunday, the day of rest. And even if they set off tomorrow they're too idle to get up early, and are bound to faff about a bit. By her calculations they've at least a day and a half head start.

At first it is the landscape they know so well, but wetter. Dawn is colourless. Creatures are hiding from the rain. The wood turns into a valley and they descend, the horses picking their way over craggy rocks bright with neon green moss. Valiant's hooves slip occasionally in the stodge of mud. 'You can do it,' Roan says, stroking her grey neck. He loves riding. He can't help enjoying it, the warm strong body underneath him.

Finally, they get to the outer limit of what they know. The lake in which the enchantress Vivien, the Lady of the Lake, is meant to live in her underwater queendom. People say she and Merlin loved each other once, but she left him. Rumour has it she wanted to know all his spells and got angry when he wouldn't give them to her; that his broken heart is why he hates women and witches.

Elva and Roan dismount to have breakfast and sit under a willow by the banks of the lake, watching the grey water pock with raindrops and the geese squabble in the reeds. They eat some bread and cheese. Elva lies down for a few minutes in the speckled silence.

'Is your back hurting already?' Roan asks.

'It's always hurting,' she says through teeth.

They barely speak for a quarter of an hour, as though both suddenly shy with each other, slightly embarrassed by what they think they are doing. Roan watches a crow watch him. And then Elva says: 'Can you help me mount Goldentrot again? Probably easier if you help.' He gives her a lift up. 'Right,' she says. 'Thanks. I guess we just have to work out where King Pelles' castle is now.'

'You don't have a map?' Roan asks, looking worried.

'No, do you have a map?' she snaps.

'I just thought—'

'What, that I'd think of everything? I couldn't get one, alright? But I've sneaked into Merlin's library plenty of times. It's how I taught myself to read. He hardly uses it, you know, all those massive tomes covered in dust.' Roan shivers. Books give him the creeps. He's heard a single one can be made from the scraped skin of over a hundred calves. 'Anyway,' Elva says. 'The point is I've seen plenty of maps of Britain.'

'Which way, then?' Roan asks.

'Erm, well…'

Luckily, the argument does not escalate too much

before there is a splash. It looks for a moment like a strange goose has emerged from the water with a long neck. But then they realise it is a shining woman's arm, and an elegant finger is pointing north.

Roan stares with disbelief. The actual Lady of the Lake!

'Thanks, Vivien!' Elva shouts at the hand. 'Don't worry, we're going to get the grail before Merlin,' and the Lady in the Lake gives her the thumbs-up.

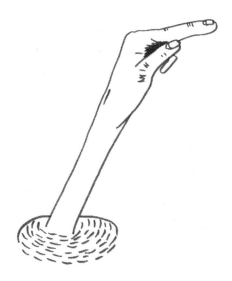

VIII

The further from the castle they get, the wilder the land seems. Fewer trees have been chopped down to make good hunting grounds; fewer animals have been hunted. Everything brims with life – soon every inch of it seems to be wriggling or buzzing. There are patches of gorse with its flame-gold flowers, and brambles jewelled with juicy blackberries. Badgers snuffle in the sallow.

As the woods get thicker, woodpeckers hammer. Elva and Roan pick through the trees on their steeds and startle those water-spirits, Morgens, who are combing their blue hair beside a waterfall. They pass a little herd of fauns – hairy-legged goat-people with horns, who will eat literally anything – that scatter.

Roan is excited by what he sees at first: 'Look, Elva,' he keeps saying, 'that jay's wrestling a worm' or 'look at all this mistletoe!' But as the afternoon darkens and they get further from his family, the creaks and rustles of the woods begin to put him on edge.

Also, the longer they ride in silence the more time Roan has to worry. 'We should have packed a sword,' he says suddenly, peering at a puddle that could be a vast pawprint.

'You what?' Elva asks, irritably.

'A sword. There are wolves and bears. I've heard about the dogheaded beasts and the giant-cat monsters… Didn't Sir Kay hunt one that had slaughtered 180 warriors and was kind of half-fish?'

'Can you use a sword, Roan?' Elva asks him, impatient.

'No,' Roan admits. 'I hate them.'

'Then what use would it be?' she asks. 'Are you, who loves animals more than anyone I know and would probably hold a sword like it's a dirty spoon, seriously going to kill a wolf with one?'

'No,' he admits, quickly, his brow crinkling. Repulsed by the idea. 'Never.'

'Well then,' Elva says. 'Look, Roan,' she adds, 'did you not see those Morgens jump? Those fauns scatter? We're from Camelot. Our cloaks, the insignia on the horses…'

'You mean they're scared of *us*?' Roan half-snorts through his nose. It's such a silly idea. 'But. But the knights of the round table are the protectors of the land. Camelot always defends them against—'

'Against what, Roan?' Elva asks. 'It's the people of Camelot who come to the woods to hunt and kill. Do you realise that bad guys always think they're good?'

'But. But there *are* fearsome monsters in this forest, right?' Roan asks, his head spinning. Surely something he has been taught is true. And how does Elva know so much stuff?

'*We're* the monsters,' Elva says.

As if to illustrate her point, just ten minutes later their horses step into a little clearing that has a huge oak in it, and they can see at once it is an elf tree full of little rooms, all lit up by glow-worms in the dusk. The tree is a hive of activity. Some of the elves are drinking droplets of dew and roasted rosehips, perched on milkcaps in the leaf mould. Others knock dust off the autumn leaves they use as rugs, or clean their acorn-shell hats, or play with their pet snails. A bat and some tits are roosting in the crevices. Two tiny elves play catch with a holly berry.

'AAAAAAAGGGHHHHHHH!' the bearded elf who is in charge of lookout shouts. 'KNIGHTS ON ENORMOUS CHOMPY KILLER HORSES!!' There is a communal gasp, and in a moment twenty tiny doors in the tree slam shut.

'We're not—' Roan begins. 'Hang on, wait—' And then Goldentrot leans in to chomp some grass and stomps on their milkcap stools. 'Oh, sorry, yeah he is a bit clumsy—'

'Leave them alone,' Elva says.

'No,' Roan says. He wants to look at them. He's never seen an elf tree in the wild – they are such intricate nests. But also, he doesn't like people not liking

40

him. He wants to convince them he's good. He dismounts then walks toward the tree with his hands up. 'I'm not a knight,' he says, 'Please. We're not knights. We don't have swords. We like elves.'

A tiny door opens, and an old elf with white hair pops his head out and shakes his fist at them. 'Oh yes, that's right,' he says. 'I'm sure you find us very cute and amusing. Like you all found poor Tom Thumb!'

'Tom Thumb?' Roan asks.

'My poor brother,' the elf says. 'But why would you have heard of him? What's a poor elf's struggle to you lot? Tom was no bigger than your thumb. One hot day he went for a swim in the river and was swallowed whole by a fish. That fish was served up to King Arthur, and when they cut it open Tom jumped out. That brute Arthur went to eat him – we know you eat every living creature in Camelot – so Tom did a little jig to distract him, then tripped over a fork. Anyway, Arthur chortled, and said: 'This dumb little Tom Thumb is so amusing I will spare him and he can be my jester forever!"

'That's not nice,' Roan says.

'No. No it isn't, is it! And every night after that for a whole year, Tom Thumb had to wear a tiny jester's hat and perform on the round table during the feast – tapdancing, juggling peas, pratfalls, cartwheels, gags – whilst those evil knights belly-laughed, until he could stand it no more and tried to escape on the back of one of the kitchen rats. Alas, he was caught in a rat-trap and is now in Camelot's dungeons.'

'That's awful,' Roan says. 'Poor Tom! I'm so sorry. I wish I could help, but I'm just a housemaid's son, I mean—'

'We'll help,' Elva says. 'We're on our way to get the Holy Grail before the knights do. We want to teach them a lesson, that they can't just take everything for themselves. And when we get back to Camelot, we're going to open those dungeons.'

'Are you kidding me?' Roan asks, suddenly getting the sinking feeling that Elva has gone completely mad. 'I'm not teaching anyone a lesson – I just want my mum to be well.'

'Other people have families too!' Elva says, indignantly. 'This elf has a brother who is wrongly imprisoned!'

'Okay,' Roan says, putting his dark head of hair in his hands. 'Okay, of course I want to help. I mean, if there's a chance I'll try. It's just, I'm only the dog boy—' He hears a small door creak open, and then another.

'These two humans actually seem alright,' an elf's voice says.

'Yes, I think they're our friends,' says another.

'Thanks,' says Roan, because he really needed to hear that.

IX

That night they camp by the elf tree.

Roan goes for a forage. The sky has cleared and churns thickly with stars, billions of them, the constellations named for gods and kings, and all the infinite shining nameless ones. The full moon has a crust of frost. Picking through the branches and thorns he manages to collect lots of sweet chestnuts, that he cooks over a fire to supplement their bread and cheese, and blackberries for pudding. These are to share with the elves, as picking blackberries from sharp brambles is obviously extremely dangerous work for little people. Soon everyone has juice-stained faces.

The elves help Elva. One, a female elf called Buttercup, shows her a tiny map as big as a postage stamp, which Elva copies out on a larger scale in glow-worm light, dipping her little finger in blackberry juice and smearing it on a big leaf. It's not the best map, but Elva thinks she gets the basic idea.

They'll be going through giant country, aiming for a small river called Barking Beck, which they will follow to Dungeon Gill, a steep ravine between two mountains. In the valley there are dangerous knights, including, rumour has it, an extremely wicked rogue knight called Tarquin, and another group who have captured many princesses and imprisoned them in the Castle of Maidens. There's also a beast along the way. And possibly a dragon or two. ('And that's assuming no baby dragons recently,' Buttercup notes.) Then, the faerie folk say, England splutters out into a wasteland of blackened marsh, within which is King Pelles' poisoned kingdom, Carbonek.

At bedtime, Roan and Elva sleep in their clothes under a blanket she's brought, but it's still cold. Buttercup sees them shivering in the night, the cold catching Roan's cough, and piles some leaves on top of them for an extra layer.

Roan wakes up and a crow is looking straight at them. He watches the crow watch them. He gets a weird feeling it's the same crow from the lake. 'Elva,' he says, sitting up, and the crow flaps away as the leaves slide off him.

'Hhmm,' Elva says, waking up slowly in the dawn light. 'Oh,' she says, remembering everything. She grins. The forest chirps and babbles around her as she stretches her arms, which are speckled like eggshells.

There is a slug clinging to the underside of her foot. 'Your pet?' she asks an elf-child, plucking it off.

'Naughty Glop!' the elf-child tells her slug.

After some more bread they say their goodbyes and thankyous, and Elva makes more unrealistic promises.

Roan helps her up onto Goldentrot and mounts Valiant and they set off. As the day wears on he gets more nervous – they are heading into giant country. Elva is buzzing, and as blasé as ever. 'I bet they're just as lovely as the elves,' she says.

'What about that terrible one King Arthur had to battle with in Morgannwg? Cribwr the Giant. I remember John the groom telling me that tale.'

'Go on then, Roan, tell me the story,' Elva says.

'What, now?' Roan asks, watching her horse lift its tail and tumble dung out onto the floor.

'Yep, why not? We've got all day.'

'Okay, so, the Giant was as tall as a castle turret, with legs like tree trunks and fists like boulders, and a cape made from the beards of kings. He refused to recognise Arthur as his king, and in fact tried to pin him down and shear his beard off. Arthur was so furious he went and found the giant's three sisters and played a trick on them.'

'What sort of trick?'

'Well,' Roan explains, trying to remember the details, 'he told the first sister he was called Hot Stew, the second sister he was called Warm Porridge, and the third he was called – what was it? Oh yeah, A Morsel of Bread.'

'Interesting,' Elva says. 'And why did he do that?'

'Erm,' Roan says, losing confidence in the tale now. He's sure it was really funny when John told it –

everyone in the stables was in fits of giggles. 'When the first sister shouted 'Help me! Hot Stew is attacking me!', the giant just answered 'Let it cool'. And when the second sister shouted 'This Warm Porridge is smothering me!', the giant answered 'Leave some for later, then.' And when the third sister called out 'A Morsel of Bread is choking me!', Cribwr the Giant answered, 'Take a smaller piece, you idiot."

'Oh, I remember now,' Elva says, having actually known the story all along. 'It's the amusing anecdote where our king murders three women.'

'You knew it already?' Roan says, a bit sulkily, feeling small. If she knows everything maybe he shouldn't bother speaking at all. 'Why did you make me say it all, then?'

'Do tell me,' Elva says. 'Why does this story make you frightened of giants and not of our king the serial killer? I'm all ears…'

And then there is the most enormous, bone-shaking, earth-shaking THUD, and then louder: THUD, THUD, THUD.

The horses rear and the calm puddles smash and the birds hurl themselves out of trees to cloud the skies with shrieking, and all the creatures of the earth leap into their burrows and tunnels and hide from the ginormous footsteps which are coming towards them.

X

Now, perhaps you have already heard the famous tale of Sir Gawain and the Green Knight? Many poets better than I have told the story, so I'll keep to the important facts.

One New Year's Day in Camelot, around the year Roan was born, King Arthur's court was exchanging lavish gifts like goblets that spelt out 'Best Knight Ever' in jewels and waiting for the eighteenth course of their feast, a cockentrice with all the trimmings (a beast that's half cockerel, half suckling pig), when the king asked to hear of an amazing adventure. 'Come on, which of you can tell me the greatest story?'

At that moment a huge gust of wind flung the great doors open, and in rode a green giant in green armour on a green horse. His face was nearly as big as the round table itself, tattooed with elaborate patterns. His vast beard seemed needled like a pine tree. He carried an axe.

'Fee-fi-ho-ho,' he said. 'I'll give you a good story. 'I've come from the wildwood for a Christmas game. You may strike me once with an axe, on the condition that I may return the blow in a year and a day. The prize is this beautiful axe, as we know you love axes.'

49

'Hmm. That *is* a beautiful axe,' Arthur said, sucking the brains out of a red squirrel. 'If one of my brave knights was to win that for me, that would be a great gift.'

Most of the knights were a few meads down so hesitated to volunteer, but Sir Gawain, Arthur's nephew, said: 'Why not, I'll do it!' He stood up, oozing confidence, as he fancied himself with an axe.

The giant bent to his knees and bared his vast neck. Gawain, nearly feeling sorry for the poor lunk, raised the weapon up high and slammed it down with merciless accuracy, neatly beheading him with a single stroke. He waited for his fellow knights to whoop and cheer with approval.

But, get this – the Green Knight's body didn't slump. Instead, he stretched out his arm, picked up the mossy crag of his head by the hair, dripping with green blood, and hopped back onto his emerald steed. 'See you at the Green Chapel next year,' the head told Gawain. 'I'll be waiting for you in a year and a day. The forest folk are looking forward to seeing me chop down a knight of the round table,' and off he galloped.

It was a pretty good trick. Gawain spent the rest of the year scared out of his wits. And even though (spoiler alert) the Green Knight actually let Gawain off from being beheaded in the end, after many scrapes and adventures, he was certainly made to have a long hard think about what he'd done.

Anyway, the reason I'm telling you this is because the giant thudding towards Elva and Roan right now is that very same Green Knight. You know, the one you can't kill. And look, he's furious, yelling:

'Who from Camelot DARES to enter the LAND OF THE GIANTS after that lesson I taught you?'

He beats the cliff of his chest, and roars a roar that makes all the canopy shudder like fear. The children try to turn their horses, but Elva is not an experienced rider and Goldentrot bucks her off.

Elva begins to run, but her crutches are in the saddlebag and she trips over her own foot, head over heels. She grunts with anger at herself: 'UGH! Stupid lopsided legs!'

'Elva!' Roan pulls his reins hard and jumps off to help her, only for the giant to lift Elva up by the belt. She writhes like a fly caught in a thread of spider's web. The Green Knight booms:

'Why are you here? Did that ROTTEN COURT send you to bring MORE

DEATH? They will *never* tame giants. We will *never* bow to their laws! Don't they understand nature is stronger than their AXES?'

Roan looks him in the huge green pool of his eye. The giant's shouty words *sound* scary, but are they? He's against death. Against axes. Something clicks into place.

'Please,' Roan says, deciding to be brave. 'Could you put my friend down? She has a bad back.'

'Sorry?' the Green Knight asks, altogether less boomily.

'If you wouldn't mind.'

'Hang on, aren't you meant to stab my ankles with your tiny swords, which remind me slightly of splinters, and send tiny arrows into my eyes, which really irritates me like when you get an eyelash in your eye?'

'Elva hates Camelot,' Roan says, then adds, realising it's true: 'I think I hate Camelot too. Well, except my mum and sister, but they just work there, and I'm sure they'd leave if given a chance. I think – I think we're on the same side. We're trying to get the grail before the knights do. My mum's ill and we hear it can heal people.'

52

The Green Knight appears to think for a moment. The leafy tattoos on his face crinkle with thought, and then he carefully lays Elva down.

'Alright then. Let's see. A test. Or no, let's call it a game. I like games! Tie up your horses and follow me.'

Roan ties up the horses and gets Elva her crutches, and they follow the giant towards a green hill. It only takes three steps for him, but it takes them a brisk ten minutes. When they arrive they realise it's not a hill but a huge green castle, guarded by a babbling brook that serves as a moat, and a fence of holly and thistle. The turrets are covered entirely with a tangle of ivy and briar rose and honeysuckle.

The giant leads them to a flowerbed near the door. There is a flower that Roan has never seen before.

'My home,' the Green Knight says. 'But before you may cross the threshold, the test. Here before you is a very rare and magical flower, the lesser-scented ghost-bell. It blooms all year round, even through the snow. It is night-scented, and its haunting fragrance gives those who inhale it the ability to see what is invisible until the dawn. Its head will always point the way you need to go. You may take it with you, erm – what were your names again?'

'Elva and Roan,' Elva says, still getting her breath back.

'You may take it with you, Elva and Roan, on the

condition that what is done to the flower today will be done to you in a year and a day.'

'Right,' says Elva. 'Can we take a moment?'

'Of course,' the Green Knight says.

Elva takes Roan aside. 'It sounds like it might be worth having,' she says. 'We only have a blackberry juice map on a crumbling leaf, so it might show us the way more accurately, and seeing what is invisible could be super-useful if we're looking for the Holy Grail. I've heard stories that it's only revealed to those without sin and that sort of thing. So I'm thinking, maybe we pull this flower out by the roots? Because I don't really care if we get uprooted from Camelot in a year and a day. We don't want to snap the stalk, because that might mean they break our legs or our backs, and my back is certainly broken enough already, and beheading is a no-no, so...'

'No,' Roan says, and he realises that just this once Elva doesn't have all the answers. He does, though. He knows flowers. 'Any way you pick it is likely to kill it,' he says. 'I won't kill a rare flower. It's precious.'

'Oh,' Elva says, irritably. 'So it's a trap? Just another trick? There's no way of winning, then?'

But Roan is going back over to the lesser-scented ghostbell. He looks very carefully at the leaves, which are toothed and heart-shaped; at the slender gold pedicel attaching the bell; the pale blue dots on the

54

silver petals. Then he looks up at the giant. 'I've taken it now,' Roan says. 'I'm going to carry the flower in my memory, and if I see ever another one I'll know that day is a lucky day.'

The Green Knight smiles back warmly and nods. 'Well done, Roan,' he says. 'You won, friend. You won! And I will carry you in my memory. In a year and a day I will come and see you, and take in the wonderful young man you will become.'

XI

Roan and Elva spend the night in the green castle, where they are made very welcome.

Everything in there is, of course, absolutely vast. At dinner a slither has to be carved for them from a planetary dumpling, to be washed down with a thimbleful of ale. The delicious apple pie for desert is so humungous that Elva trips in whilst leaning over to taste it and gets rather gooey, which makes all the giants chuckle.

The hall is decked with boughs and heated by a gargantuan fire that makes Roan's cheeks burn. He has to screen his eyes to look at it, like it's a domesticated sun. After dinner the harp comes out, and there is dancing. Elva says she's probably safer just watching and Roan wonders if he's supposed to say 'Come on, try, it'll be fun', but decides it's best not to push it, and gamely jigs around a pepper-pot partner.

At bedtime, baths are run for them in colossal teacups. They read a story from a book of giants' faerietales, turning each page like a door, then sleep that night in the fluffy slippers of the Green Knight's wife.

In the morning, they wake up when the Green Knight's wife forgetfully starts slipping her feet into the slippers. Luckily, their hair tickles her toes. 'Pardon me!' she says. 'Oh goodness, what a way to wake up!'

To make up for it, she fusses around generously and gives Roan and Elva immense crumbs of bread and cheese to replenish their saddlebags. The Green Knight tells them they will be safe in their travels through the Land of the Giants, and to remember to keep their eyes out for the lesser-scented ghostbell. They thank him and set out on their way.

There are quite a lot of hills in the Land of the Giants, and you always have to double-check before you start to climb them in case they're actually a giant having a nap (at one point they embarrassingly confuse a nostril for a cave). Otherwise, it's a good day's riding, with paths that are wide and easy as long as you watch out for the occasional ditch of a footprint. 'We should make the beck by evening,' Elva says.

'Why do you think it's called Barking Beck?' Roan asks. His dark curls have gone a bit fluffy and wild, as he so rarely washes his hair. 'Do you think that's where the beast is? The elves mentioned a beast.'

'Let's just wait and see,' Elva says, riding ahead of him, her own hair shining like rose gold. 'There's no point worrying about something that might not be there. Hey, I was impressed by how you solved that puzzle last night, by the way. It was almost like a riddle, wasn't it? I like riddles. There's lots of them in Merlin's library. Guess this one: *I am a fine warrior, but I only grow bright between two mute creatures, and any woman can tame me if she looks after me and feeds me properly.'*

'Mmm… tricky. Oh, I've got it. Fire! The mute creatures are the stones you bang together to make a spark, right?'

'You're good! How about this one: *I am water become bone.'*

'Err… ice?'

'Yep. Two points! Okay, next…'

They pass the afternoon pleasantly with this game, riddling and making up their own riddles, but by evening Roan's anxiety mounts. They are close enough to Barking Beck to hear it hushing them when they decide to stop for the night, but the fire he makes and the blanket no longer seem enough. The temperature is dropping rapidly. In the night he wakes shivering, his jaw aching from clenching it. Everything is horribly pale, every leaf and grass blade seems dipped in salt, and a terrible phantom mist begins to creep in from somewhere and swirl around them. He realises Elva's lips are blue. *I am water become bone…*

They've set out on this quest to save someone's life. It would be so ugly and ridiculous if they just died too. He gives Elva his half of the blanket, carefully folding it over her, and paces until dawn, rubbing his hands together and missing the warmth of the kennel. They will have to start finding caves or make camps, or they will simply freeze to death on a night any colder.

And what is that bloodcurdling howling, barking noise? Wolves, surely. But like no wolves he's ever heard.

XII

At breakfast Roan is grumpy. He doesn't say much. Just: 'The crow is there.'

'What crow?' Elva asks. 'I honestly haven't seen this crow.'

'It's behind you,' Roan says, because it is, a glossy carrion crow tilting its head.

'Um, okay,' Elva says, but of course by the time she's turned around it isn't. She shrugs. 'Look, I'm not questioning that you're seeing crows, Roan. It's a fairly unremarkable occurrence. I'm just questioning whether it's actually the same crow rather than, you know, a series of generic and ultimately interchangeable crows.' Roan can't believe how well-rested she seems. She hasn't even noticed he gave her his half of the blanket, which makes him grumpier.

'Fine,' he says. 'Ignore me.'

Elva goes to the toilet behind a bush, and then they mount the horses and set off again.

The mist is still hanging heavily. After pushing up the hill for half an hour, they arrive at the top and look out at the most stupendous view of – oh.

'I've never seen such an amazing boring view of nothing at all,' Roan says.

'Yes, this is the most breathtakingly unbelievable view of zero,' Elva says, getting the giggles.

'It was definitely worth the climb to see all this diddly-squat.'

But then, amazingly, the sun does start to burn through, and the mist begins to silently, rapidly lift. And the view really does become stupendous and unbelievable. Roan almost gasps. Within minutes they can see the ancient rainforest for miles in one direction, and in the other the indigo mountains they must ride towards. Before them is grassland on which herd after herd are grazing in the scraps and pools of mist: vast-shouldered musk ox and reindeer, and a herd of nearly fifty white unicorns, some of which drink palely from the beck. A kingfisher zigzags past like a jewel. And then something else flies past, the brilliant blue of a dragonfly but with a leisurely flap, flap, flap of wings.

'A wyvern!' Roan exclaims. Wyverns are small members of the dragon family that breathe frost instead of fire. He has never seen one before and can't believe it. 'An actual wyvern!' he says. 'They're so rare. Elva, Elva, look! Look at that wyvern!' It lands on the riverbank and then breathes a sparkly cloud at the water, before pulling out its catch: a water rat it begins to peck at with its beaky mouth. 'Did you see that, Elva?' Roan asks. 'That's how it catches its food – by freezing it! It's like a rat lolly. I can't believe I just saw that…'

'Wow,' Elva says. 'Wow.'

All morning they ride on, soaking it all in, stopping to watch birds, otters and wyverns, grinning at each other. Occasionally though, they start to notice other things in the bushes too. Makeshift tents; a pair of feet under a tatty blanket. Signs of people.

Eventually they pass a family who look like they are boiling up some nettles for a very meagre breakfast. They have the same reddish hair and colouring as Elva, and their clothes are poor and dirty. The son, who is Roan's age, has no shoes on. 'Hi,' Elva says to them.

'Elva, don't,' Roan says.

'Don't what?' Elva asks, and she shouts at the family this time: 'HI THERE!'

'Hi,' says the boy.

'What are you doing here?' Elva asks him.

'You can't ask people that,' Roan says, embarrassed.

'It's alright,' the boy says. 'You should know if you're riding that way yourselves. We're refugees from Carbonek. That's why we look such a bunch of draggles. It used to be lush – we farmed there, but it's a wasteland now. All the crops have failed, and the water has turned to poison. Everyone's dying of hunger and thirst. Some people we knew decided to escape by boat, but we didn't have enough money to pay for a place on board and we've heard about the sea-monsters too. Towards the border there's a war on, so we came through Dungeon Gill. My big sister got caught, though. She's trapped in the Castle of Maidens now.'

'I'm sorry,' Elva says. 'That doesn't sound good.'

The boy tells them the whole story: how the castle is owned by seven brothers. They were once given the prophecy that a maiden who lived at another castle would undo them all. This premonition so alarmed the brothers that they started capturing every maiden they could find, under the guise of 'rescuing' them, then forced the maidens to live in their castle instead. 'We hear there are more than twenty imprisoned there now.'

'Don't worry,' Elva says. 'We'll save your sister.'

'What?' Roan says. 'Elva, we can't just promise to –'

'Thank you,' the boy says. 'Are you from Camelot? My dad kept saying knights from Camelot would come and save us, although I was expecting grown men to be honest. We're heading to Camelot now, so they can give us refuge and a new home. I can't wait to get there! Dad says they protect everyone.'

'Um,' Roan says. 'Maybe – I mean, we are from Camelot, but we're not knights. I'm sure the knights will probably, I mean—' But the reassuring words turn to ash in his mouth and make him cough. He can't imagine King Arthur giving refuge to anyone. Outsiders are usually called traitors and thrown in the dungeon.

'If I were you I'd try the Land of the Giants first,' Elva says. 'They're really friendly; massive pies. By the way, did you pass Tarquin the rogue knight? Do you have any useful information?'

'Yep. His tower is the one with a tree outside that's decorated with the helmets and weapons of all the knights he's captured, and there are a *lot*,' the boy tells them. 'He keeps the knights as slaves. There's this copper basin outside too that says:

> *Who valueth not his life a whit,*
> *Let him this magic basin hit.*

'Anyone who hits it automatically challenges him to a battle, and Tarquin always wins. We managed to get past when he was fighting someone else. It looked brutal.'

Roan shudders.

'Thanks,' Elva says, giving the boy some bread and cheese. 'Here, take this for your family. You must need a decent breakfast.'

Roan and Elva ride on, and she hands out more

bread and cheese to other refugees they pass. After about the third time, Roan says: 'That's enough, Elva. I don't want to sound selfish, but we're about to ride into a desolate wasteland. We might need some bread and cheese ourselves.' Elva doesn't want to tell him that that was all of it.

Roan doesn't have time to worry about that anyway. All morning he has almost forgotten about the bloodcurdling howling, barking noise from last night, as he's been too excited by all the amazing wildlife. If he has thought of it for a brief moment he's written it off as a hallucination brought on by tiredness, or just a wolf, and definitely, certainly not anything bigger and scarier than that. But now he hears that bloodcurdling howling, barking noise again.

It is a kind of howl and a woof in one. A howoof, if you like. But like a whole pack of beasts is making the noise in perfect unison.

'Did you—' Roan begins.

'Yep,' Elva says.

Valiant seems nervous, like she wants to bolt. Roan holds the reins a little tighter. 'Easy, girl,' he says gently in her ear. 'We'll be fine.' There is another howoof. Closer now. 'You don't suppose,' Roan says, 'that's what a wild questing beast sounds like, do you?'

'The questing beast gets its name from the great noise it emits from its belly, a barking like *thirty*

hounds questing, or at least that's what it says in that big bestiary book in Merlin's library,' Elva tells him. 'It also says the questing beast has the head and neck of a snake, the body of a leopard, and the haunches of a lion and the feet of a deer, which sounds very unlikely, especially the snake bit, because reptiles are cold-blooded and I don't think they could mix with a... Oh. On second thoughts, it's an extraordinarily accurate description.'

Because there it is: directly in front of them, staring from black slits in green pearls. A forked tongue flickers in and out. The baying of its stomach grows louder.

Its muscular, spotted body is preparing to leap.

XIV

'D-d-did the book say if the questing beast had the head of a *poisonous* snake?' Roan asks in a whisper, looking into the wicked beads of its eyes.

'Don't remember,' Elva whispers back apologetically.

'The best thing to do if you encounter a snake is turn around and walk away,' Roan says.

'Erm, go on, then,' Elva says, looking much less confident than usual. But Roan doesn't.

'What about big cats?' he says. 'It's part lion and leopard, isn't it? I've met a few lynxes. The main thing to remember if you encounter a big cat is *never* to turn around and walk away.'

'Right. Plan B then?'

'You have to maintain eye contact,' Roan says, looking into those ghastly pupils. 'Make yourself as big as you can.' He puffs up his skinny chest a little; attempts to flex his thin, tan arms. Elva tries to sit a little straighter in her saddle.

'Snakes don't like vibrations,' he remembers, facts returning to him from past encounters in the woods. 'We could make some noise.'

'Go on then,' Elva says.

'But if you shout at big cats you must never betray even a hint of nervousness in your voice.'

'Okay, so go on then,' Elva says, impatient now for this to be over already.

The questing beast takes a step towards them. It bares its fangs. 'Um, I think I might betray a hint of nervousness in my voice,' Roan admits.

At that moment the questing beast's stomach makes that terrible howoofing noise again, like it is ravenously hungry. Its snake neck pulls back, about to spring forward and attack. Roan screws up his eyes, unable to look, even though he's meant to maintain eye contact.

And then, suddenly, the questing beast startles and bounds away on its deer feet. Another noise has frightened it, frightening the children too. It is the sound of a pack of knights galloping towards them, blowing their hunting horns.

Now, you may well be wondering how the knights of the round table caught up so quickly. They only set off this very morning, after a full English breakfast with boar's bacon, swan sausage and a great auk's egg. But, unfortunately for Roan and Elva, they soon decided to make a race of it. 'Let's spice this boring quest up,' Sir Lionel said by the lake. 'Last one to the grail is a big fat tallowcatch.'

'You mean a big girl,' barked Sir Bors.

68

'How dare you insult the fairer species, Sir Bors?' Lancelot asked. 'I will get there first for the honour of the female sex.' (He didn't notice that the Lady of the Lake was giving him a thumbs down.)

'This grail's mine,' Sir Lionel bragged, pulling down the visor on his freshly polished helmet. 'May the race commence.'

'Gentlemen, I think you're forgetting that it was me who heroically volunteered for the honour of this grail quest, after you'd all drunk rather too much mead,' Sir Galahad piped up.

And then they kicked their horses hard with their spurs and galloped off, not worrying about trampling on a few nests and a bit of elf furniture or a refugee's tent or two along the way.

Knowing that the knights are only minutes from catching up with them, Roan and Elva gallop on themselves, as fast as Goldentrot and Valiant can go. They hear rowdy cries from behind:

'A questing beast over there!'

'We must vanquish this devil from the land!'

'Murder that monster!'

'It would make a great trophy for the Great Hall...'

'Guinevere would be impressed.'

'There's a ballad in this, boys! 'Questing beast' rhymes with 'roasted feast'!'

'Let me stab it!'

'Let's shoot it with an arrow first, dear brother.'

'Then I'll stab it.'

'TALLY HO!'

The cries fall further behind as the knights pursue the beast into the open grassland, sending the herds stampeding and scattering.

'Poor thing,' Roan shouts over to Elva as they gallop breathlessly on, the wind pouring through Valiant's silver mane into his face. 'They shouldn't kill such a rare animal. I mean, I know it was scary and nearly ate us, but it was just being a questing beast, wasn't it?'

'They're just being knights of the round table too, I guess,' Elva shouts back over the hooftaps, her eyes flashing with anger. 'Just being arrogant, privileged, violent men. As they always say at Camelot, *boys will be boys.*' Her eyes flicker over to Roan's face, which she sees crumple. 'Oh, I mean – I didn't mean you, Roan, obviously. You're different from the other boys. You know I didn't mean you, right? You're nice.'

The path narrows and they have to gallop in single file for a few minutes. She can't see his face. Roan thinks about the other boys in Camelot and how he hates them too. He thinks about this quest and how if the knights find out what they are doing and catch them they will throw him and Elva in a dungeon. Or they will spike his head outside Camelot as a warning, like Pierce spears the tender bodies of frogs.

'I know,' he says to her, after a while, when they slow for the horses to pick their way down a slope. 'I know you didn't mean me.'

'The actual law of this land says if a married woman goes off with another man, the husband shall take all her property and she is to *lose her nose and ears*,' Elva says, the angry rant in her head running on. 'They're just shameless.'

'Ugh,' Roan says. 'I can't believe the knights are so fast, though. How was I ever stupid enough to think we could beat them? They have faster stronger horses, and they're experienced riders. We're never going to get the grail before them now. We've no chance – maybe we should give up and go home.'

'No,' Elva snaps, the fury definitely directed at him this time. 'No way. I'm going to pretend you didn't say that. After everything we've been through?'

Roan feels the tears brimming in his eyes. He swallows, swallows.

'Look, did you see how easily distracted they were from their path?' Elva says. 'That's a really good sign. Come on, we can do this, Roan, I know we can. We're just going to have to be a bit inventive with the distractions we put in their way.'

'Alright,' he says. 'Alright.'

'Ooh, talking of distractions, I have an idea.' Elva winces a little as she says this, pain dampening her exhilaration.

'Do you need to lie down?'

'Yes,' Elva says, 'Always. But it's not safe yet. We need to get to Dungeon Gill before nightfall. Come on.'

XV

Soon the mountains grow close and the path narrows.

The walls close in. Everything is chill and shadowy in the ravine. There are little caves in the sides hung with bats and stinking of damp. The rocks are jagged.

Ahead of them in the centre of their path, where they cannot avoid it, is the rogue knight Tarquin's fearful tower. It is skinny and sharp. The dank walls loom, decorated with the shields of every knight Tarquin has ever captured. Each one shows a coat of arms: a unique design representing a noble British family. Quartered shields with castles and roses; unicorns and rampant lions.

If you listen carefully, there is a sound like men in dungeons moaning under your feet.

On the oak tree's bare branches perch a murder of crows, croaks spilling from their dark throats. The tree is hung with horrible weapons. Longswords, shortswords, knives, axes with crusted red edges, bludgeons, clubs, war hammers, man catchers, maces, halberds, lances, forks, pikes, slings, sharpened poles, bows, arrows, morning stars of brutal spikes that drip fresh blood onto the tree's tangle of roots. A tree of pain.

Roan feels his head start to spin; that clammy panic. Large, dark, razor-toothed fish move slowly in the moat's dark waters like shadows.

Roan's face grows greyer, and he bites his lip. 'I'm scared,' he tells Elva. There is an ominous silence. Tarquin is nowhere to be seen. The copper basin gleams like a wet mouth. It swims with letters. Roan sees Elva is reading the words again, her lips moving as she whispers them to herself. When she's finished, she looks up at him.

'It's pretty ugly, isn't it?' Elva agrees. 'All the time and money and thought these men put into different ways to wound people. But don't worry: I have a brilliant plan. You just have to follow me. Ready?' Roan gulps. But he looks into his friend's serious, kind face and he decides to trust her.

'Ready.'

'Giddy up, Goldentrot!' Elva gives Goldentrot's haunch a swift kick and they begin to gallop again, quickly.

Roan and Valiant set off in hot pursuit. He closes his eyes, hanging on tight to Valiant's neck, wishing the moment was over, his heart thudding in his chest as they approach the tree. He feels one of its branches brush his arm like a spindly finger. They ride right up to the tower and then—

They ride right past the tower.

'Oh,' says Roan, about five minutes later when they are well clear. 'I see.'

'It's pretty simple, really,' Elva says. 'Just don't strike the basin.'

'I didn't think of that.'

'It was all in that silly rhyme in the end. How did it go again?

Who valueth not his life a whit,
Let him this magic basin hit,
He is an utter twit.'

And then they hear a loud, sonorous ringing sound that carries through the ravine. DOOOOONNN-NGGGGGG! DOOOOOOONNNNNGGGGG!

Elva grins and punches the air. '*Yes!* They hit the basin. The knights hit the basin! I knew those knights wouldn't be able to resist the basin! They're going to be fighting Tarquin all afternoon now. YES! YOU TWITS! YOU NITWITS! Ah, I think I've earned a quick lie-down. Help me off Goldentrot, would you?'

'My pleasure,' Roan smiles, using his hands to make a step for her foot. He is still a bit shaky. 'Well done, Elva. Hey, if we're stopping shall we have some of that bread and cheese for lunch now?'

'Oh,' says Elva.

XVI

There is, of course, no bread and cheese for their lunch, as Elva gave it all away to the refugees. She lies down, looking up at the mountains and grey sky. 'Can't you just forage something?' Elva asks.

'It's nearly winter,' Roan snaps. 'We're in a sunless ravine. What were you thinking – lightly toasted bat guano on a bed of mould?'

'How about eggs? I saw something hurry into its nest just then. Well, it was more of a burrow. Or a kind of scorched hole in a split rock. It was sort of a snake, but with a white cockscomb like a cockerel. Unusual looking. It didn't see me, anyway. You could poke a stick in there, see if there's any eggs to boil...' She realises Roan's eyes are round with shock and horror.

'You want me to poke a stick in a basilisk's nest?' he yelps. 'Why don't I just try and remove a wolf's tooth with an axe and ram a pinecone up a brown bear's bottom whilst I'm at it? I'm sure they won't mind!'

'Oh, right, I do remember reading about basilisks in Merlin's bestiary, but the picture was more half-goose half-crocodile... Aren't they dangerous or something?'

'Its breath is so toxic it kills on inhalation,' Roan says. 'Its skin is so poisonous that when a knight once speared one on horseback, the poison travelled up the spear and both the man and horse fell dead. Oh, and it has such an intense fire in its gaze that if it looks on you, you die on the spot.'

'I'm not that hungry,' Elva says. 'I can last until dinner time.'

'Sorry would be nice.'

'I was just being kind to starving people,' Elva says. She's never been very good at saying sorry, as she likes always being right. 'Look, something will turn up.' Then she sees a crow crossing the clouds and there is a heavy *clonk* right next to them. 'Did that crow just drop something?'

'Yes,' Roan says. 'It's the crow that has been following us all week and it just dropped a bag right next to me. Like I said, a sorry would be nice.'

'Ooh, what's in the bag?'

'Stop changing the subject.'

'Sorry, I thought a crow dropping a bag *was* the subject.'

'You should say sorry.'

'I just said it,' Elva says, with a dismissive wave of her hand.

'Say sorry for giving away my lunch and also sorry for not believing me about the crow.'

'Come on, open the bag!'

Roan peers at the bag. It looks like it's been taken from Tarquin's tree. He undoes the buckle.

'Arrows,' Roan says, looking inside. 'That's pretty useless, since we don't have a bow. Maybe the crow just dropped it by accident.' But then he digs a little deeper and his hand brushes something. 'Hang on,' 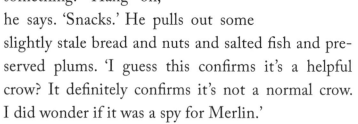 he says. 'Snacks.' He pulls out some slightly stale bread and nuts and salted fish and preserved plums. 'I guess this confirms it's a helpful crow? It definitely confirms it's not a normal crow. I did wonder if it was a spy for Merlin.'

'Unless the plums are poisonous,' Elva says. 'How about you just lick one to start.'

'Lick it yourself,' Roan snaps. Then he looks at her and they both start to giggle. They lick the plums and decide they are fine, and eat hungrily. 'I definitely need to teach you a bit more about nature,' Roan tells her after he's full. 'I can't believe you didn't recognise a basilisk. It sounds like Merlin's bestiary was written by someone who doesn't know much about animals.'

'Nonsense,' Elva says. 'It's full of great facts. Like how bees, who are obviously the smallest of birds, are born from the decaying bodies of oxen and have a king. Mice are created out of dirt. Goat-blood melts diamonds…'

Roan starts to laugh. 'Bees are birds?'

'Yep, and weasels give birth through their ears. Um. Oh. Okay,' she admits, 'maybe you're right and it's not completely trustworthy.'

After lunch they set off again, picking through the slippery ravine, passing small waterfalls and echoing caves. It only takes a couple of hours before a castle comes into view: the Castle of Maidens. Even though it's only about four o'clock, the sun is long gone behind the mountain and flaming torches have already been lit outside for evening. 'So what's the plan for this one?' Roan asks. 'I guess we just go past it again?'

'You're kidding me, right?' Elva demands, fiercely. 'Twenty girls are imprisoned in there and you just want to trot on past?'

'Elva, come on – I'm just the dog boy. I'm not a knight in shining armour.'

'You're not *just* anything,' Elva says. 'Stop putting yourself down or I'm going to start getting really annoyed with you, understand? Anyway, you don't need to be their knight in shining armour. Remember the prophecy? It said a maiden from another castle would undo the seven brothers. a.k.a. *me*.'

'You think the prophecy's about *you*?' Roan asks, getting nervous again. 'Elva, you're getting carried away. Please. You know what they do to girls. They capture them. If you get yourself locked up, I don't know what I'll do. We're nearly at Carbonek. Come on. I have to think of my mum, and Gwen, and…'

'Roan, I've got this. They won't even look at me and see a maiden. They'll just see a poor little hunchback. Now, remember what I said just before the elf-tree?'

'Erm, I would probably hold a sword like a dirty spoon?' Roan says, as he hasn't forgotten that particular burn.

'No, not that thing, the other thing,' Elva tells him. 'Bad guys always think they're good. These brothers don't think they're the bad guys, right? Every knight in existence thinks he's 'rescuing' a maiden every time he kidnaps her. They're probably totally sick of everyone acting like *they're* the bad guys. Even though they are the bad guys. Do you follow me?'

She's doing that talking-very-fast thing again. 'Not really,' Roan says.

'Help me dismount,' Elva instructs him. 'Then tether the horses and hide in the bushes. I'll soon sort this out.'

Roan helps her dismount, ties up Goldentrot and Valiant, and quietens them with a few snacks (he has to suppress his giggles when Valiant nuzzles his palm).

Then he squats behind a bush. He watches Elva as she pulls her cape over her hair like a shawl, gets her crutches, and hobbles towards the door letting her hunch show, her shoulder blade jutting forward. He sees a man open the door and speak to her with growing agitation.

Just a minute later six knights pour out of the castle, hastily putting their helmets on. They saddle up their steeds and gallop away. Once they're gone, Elva hits the last knight over the head with her crutch and he slumps unconscious to the floor.

'Hey Roan,' she shouts cheerfully. 'Come on up! All sorted. Let's tie this guy up and free the princesses, FOR I AM THE MAIDEN OF PROPHECY!! WHOOP!' She pulls the shawl off her head and her reddish hair looks molten in the light of the flaming torches, and her cheeks are flushed with happiness. Roan can hear over twenty female voices cheering and whistling and hollering inside.

He runs over with some rope from the saddlebag and starts tying the unconscious knight up whilst Elva looks for keys. 'How did you do it?' he asks her.

'I just said I'd escaped a castle where wicked knights have imprisoned twenty or so fair maidens, and I was hoping they might be kind enough to rescue them. People never recognise themselves in stories, you know.'

'And where did you direct them?' Roan says.

'Camelot, of course,' Elva replies, with a gleam in her eye.

'You shouldn't have hit this knight so hard,' Roan says, looking at a tender bruise coming up. 'You cut his cheek. It looks really painful.'

She shakes a bunch of keys. 'Sorry,' she says. 'But hey, I found these. Now, let's liberate some women!'

XVII

Soon the Castle of Maidens is full of excitement and high spirits, as all the women and girls are freed from the various turrets and rooms they've been locked up in. They spill out and hug Elva like she's a long-lost sister.

After much animated conversation, the maidens decide that, as it's pitch black outside, they'll celebrate tonight and set off for their homes in the morning. Soon a couple find a lute and a fiddle, and they're dancing and jigging and partying and jumping on the knights' beds having pillow fights.

And feasting! Because the Castle of Maidens has this most amazing magical table where food appears if you strike it, so soon they're all banging and drumming on it with fists and forks, and every time something delicious appears: a bowl of luscious out-of-season fruits like strawberries and peaches and something yellow and scaly with spiky green hair at the top; and dates, a very fancy cheeseboard, oysters, scallops, crayfish, a whole baked salmon, pastries and fritters and loaves and waffles and crepes, quince jelly, marmalade, fresh butter, custards and cherry tarts, jugs of wine and berry juices and sweet parlour spices – candied ginger and aniseed to aid digestion.

Elva and Roan fill up their bellies until they feel almost dizzy, and Roan can't help giving a little burp that he hides behind his hand. They have never had such a fancy dinner in their lives.

At first Roan feels very self-conscious amongst such company, but luckily he gets chatting to a mermaid called Pearl who sits to dine in a large bucket of water. She wears an ordinary blouse, but if you peep into the water you can see her silver tail curled and gently slapping, with a rainbow sheen like a trout's.

Pearl is homesick for the sea (should that be seasick?), and glad to find someone interested in her descriptions of it. Back then, of course, the seas weren't plundered and dredged but were still as rich as the wildwood. The mermaid tells Roan of shoals of flickering mackerel miles long, clicking dolphins, pods of fin whales and sperm whales moaning their haunting songs, spawning grounds where eggs of herring lie six feet deep, reefs of corals and sea fans and sponges and peacock worms and tickly anemones.

Pearl tells him of selkies, who often shed their sealskins to come on land and take human husbands, but who you can recognise by their webbed toes. She tells him about a winged water-horse and giant sea-monsters: whales big as cities, tentacled krakens that drag down whole ships...

Roan listens greedily. Soon Pearl is insisting that any time he visits the coast, he can summon her by weeping seven tears into the sea and she'll show him around ('Sorry that sounds a bit gloomy – it's just how it works for some reason.').

Elva finds herself talking to the Lady of Shalott (or Elaine to her friends), who had a famous poem written about her by the Victorian poet Alfred Lord Tennyson. She is wearing a ruby-coloured gown with a golden belt and is really tucking into the wine. Elaine had an awful early life, brought up in a turret just outside Camelot. Her father was a horrible bully and power-freak who kept her there by pretending there was a mysterious curse and something awful would happen if she looked directly at the world. Instead, she had to stay in her room forever with only a mirror for entertainment, in which she was allowed to watch the reflections of people passing by. She was soon half-sick of shadows.

But then, when she was sixteen, she saw Sir Lancelot in the mirror and couldn't resist a proper peek. 'He was pretty dreamy,' Elaine recalls, 'and the mirror needed a polish. I just wanted a good look.'

'I had a crush on him when I was younger too,' her friend the princess agrees. 'Puppydog eyes and that cute button nose.'

'What happened next?' Elva asks.

In Tennyson's poem he says:

> *Out flew the web and floated wide—*
> *The mirror crack'd from side to side;*
> *'The curse is come upon me,' cried*
> *The Lady of Shalott.*

In actual fact, nothing bad had happened at all. Elaine realised her dad had lied about the curse, had a massive row with him, and stormed out.

'Long story short, I found work as a lady-in-waiting in Camelot,' Elaine explains. 'But then barely a week later, me and the princess were out riding and the seven brothers snatched us. Lucky you saved us, Elva! I'll finally get to see the world outside a turret! FREEDOM! More juice and wine!' She bangs the table and more goodies appear, and everyone pauses from dancing and merriment to toast Elva.

'TO ELVA! THE MAIDEN OF PROPHECY!'

'And Roan too,' Elva says, smiling radiantly at him.

'And Roan too!' the maidens agree, clinking their goblets.

That night Roan and Elva sleep in bunks in the castle, Elva on the top and Roan on the bottom. It's warm. They're safe and full. Roan should sleep well, but he finds himself awake and anxious. Being surrounded by these women makes him think of his mum and how badly she's been treated. He wishes he could hold her. He's almost the same height as her now. He thinks about the last time he hugged her, and how she winced slightly because her chest hurt. Pain flinches through him again.

'Are you awake?' Elva whispers down, hearing him tossing and turning. 'I can't sleep either.'

'Do you miss your mum too?' Roan asks.

'No,' Elva says, her soft voice carrying down through the darkness. 'No, they – they're alright. I mean, I think my mother and father are good people. My mum was sweet with me when I was little. She liked pat-a-cake and nursery rhymes, she likes pinching baby cheeks. But – I think they wish I'd never been born, deep down. They put a brave face on it, but when I try to talk to them, really talk, you know, about anything that matters to me, they just look baffled and sad. Like I'm on a far shore and they can't hear me.'

'Oh,' Roan says. 'That's – I'm sorry. I was just missing my mum. I wondered if that was why you were awake too.'

Elva is awake because she is buzzing with happiness. How can she tell Roan that, though, when his mother is so ill? She can't tell him that today was one of the best days of her life; that the only person she cares about is lying in the bunk beneath her.

XVIII

In the morning the room is full of a very pale clean light and the silence feels thick. Roan splashes his face in water and goes to the window.

It has snowed overnight and everything outside is black and white: black ice; white ice. There are tracks: a bird's and a deer's. A little bear cub rolls playfully in the drifts as its mother tries to nudge it back towards an icicle-jawed cave. The crow watches.

Downstairs, in the busy hall, Roan and Elva eat a sumptuous breakfast from that astonishing table, and fill up their saddlebags with cheese, bread and dried fruits. The maidens are setting off, layering up in as much clothing as they can. The knights had a couple of spare horses and a covered wagon in their stable, so half are bundling into that and, once they pass through the ravine, will swerve left for the coast, where some will carry on by ship or, in Pearl's case, by swimming. Others are setting off by foot, back towards Barking Beck. Elva and Roan tell them about the Green Giant and the elf-tree, in case they are passing and need shelter or help.

Only two are foolish enough to be going straight ahead, into the wasteland around Castle Carbonek:

Roan and Elva. Everyone shudders a little when they tell them where they're going. They look like they've suddenly noticed what children their saviours are, and want to ground them or tell their parents. 'Are you *sure* that's a good idea?' Pearl says. 'Couldn't you ask a grown-up?'

All the maidens agree they've heard of crops turned to slime; tree bark scabby with lesions; rivers coated with a thick black gleam; silent skies. And worse, a dark force behind it all. Something cankered at the core. 'I'm sure your mums will be worried about you if you don't head back,' Elaine says, kind-heartedly, not realising her remark will hurt both Roan and Elva in different ways.

'Sorry,' Elva says to them all, stubbornly. 'But we're not turning back. Not until we have the grail. So I guess this is goodbye. Good luck, all of you!' And she and Roan mount their horses and trot into the tumbling snowflakes.

Within half an hour they are emerging from the ravine. Ahead is just woodland. It's hard to tell where you are in the whiteness, with a white sky. Roan's knuckles feel cold and chapped; his ears turn bright red and ring painfully. Flakes catch and melt on his long black lashes, like icy tears. He feels one trickle down his back. 'So the blackberry juice map just says straight ahead-ish?' he says. 'It feels a bit—' Then the cold catches his throat and gives him a coughing fit that sounds like a series of small explosions: *k-huh, k-huh.*

'What?'

'It's not that useful, is it, without the sun to – *k-huh, k-huh* – guide us? How do we know where straight ahead is? We could be going miles out of our way.'

'What do you want me to do about it?' Elva retorts. She's got a migraine and can't feel her toes. Snow keeps packing up Goldentrot's hooves and making him slide. The horses seem unhappy; the bits are freezing in their mouths.

They must be going the right way though, because the further they go the sicker the wood seems. Pawprints become non-existent. They pass the snow-caked bodies of scrawny boar – it's usual for some to starve over the winter, but not so early. The skeleton of a griffin, which makes Roan sad when he's never seen a living one. They cross over a slim river and it stinks.

Eventually the trees thin out and the landscape becomes even grimmer. A grey horizon appears. A leaky marsh has hardened into a rink of dark ice where otter skulls jut from stony water.

'I guess this is it,' Elva says, flatly. 'The kingdom of Carbonek. We made it. Whoo-erm-hoo.' She squints through the flurry. 'Is that—?' Far away, on that bleak horizon, is something that looks like a rotten tooth.

'It must be King Pelles' Castle.'

'The Holy Grail is meant to be there?' Roan asks. It doesn't feel right.

'I know,' Elva says. 'I was thinking that. It's something *to do* with this castle, but if they had a healing cup, why wouldn't they have healed the land? I don't think we're going to just walk in and find it there on a pedestal. There's going to be a mystery to solve.'

They stop for some food, and for Elva to rest her back, but only take a short break this time – they're aware there's hardly anything for Goldentrot and Valiant to eat. The horses have been happily grazing in the wildwood, but there is nothing to graze on here. 'Sorry it's not more,' Roan tells them, as he gives them each a measly apple to crunch. Valiant's mouth tickles his hand but he doesn't feel like giggling. Afterwards Roan and Elva remount and ride torturously on through the ugly, slippery landscape. An hour passes. Two. Three. But they never seem to get nearer to the rotten tooth.

It's like the castle is a mirage; a hallucination brought on by the cold.

At last Roan says quietly, 'It'll be dark in an hour. We need to think about making a proper camp or we'll freeze to death.' Elva doesn't reply. In her head they would get to the castle tonight. She was sure of it. That was the plan. 'Elva,' Roan says. 'Do you hear me?'

'Let's talk about it in an hour, then,' she says.

'We need to make a proper camp or we'll freeze to death. You didn't see how... how blue your lips were last time we camped outside. I had to give you my covers.'

'I know.'

'You know?' Roan asks, indignant. 'You *know*?'

'What?'

This time Roan doesn't answer. They ride on towards the receding castle in a mutual sulk. The sun starts to turn a sickly pink. This would have been farmland once, before it was abandoned. They pass an empty cart, a child's corn-dolly abandoned in it. Occasionally they pass grey plants, that look as though as they've been turned to stone – small statues of poppies and daisies. Roan brushes against a bush and it crumbles to ash.

The only waymarks in the blank fields are rare trees. Roan notes, half a mile to their right, a large hawthorn, its sparse speckle of blood-bright haws the only colour in the landscape. They approach a vast oak that is still, just, hanging onto life, though some of its branches seem dead and the few acorns left on the ground look melted and greasy. 'Right,' Roan says, suddenly decisive. 'We're camping here, that's it. I'm absolutely not going any further. I'm not doing it.' He is surprised by his own voice.

'Okay,' Elva says, surprised too.

'We can use the branches to make some kind of tent.' Roan says, jumping down to touch the bark. 'It must be a thousand years old and now it's dying.' Dark weeping patches have formed on the trunk and dried to a black crust.

But then, in the shadow of the tree, he sees something. It can't be… can it? It can't. He steps closer and it is.

The lesser-scented ghostbell, which blooms all year round even through the snow, is pushing through the white crust. Toothed, heart-shaped leaves; the slender gold pedicel attaching the bell; silver petals dotted with pale blue. The flower is pointing towards the hawthorn tree.

'The lesser-scented ghostbell,' Roan says. 'It says we need to camp at the hawthorn tonight.'

'That's half a mile in the wrong direction,' Elva says. 'I thought you were absolutely not going any further.'

'That's the way we need to go,' Roan says, remembering the Green Giant's words. 'And it's night-scented, isn't it? Its fragrance gives those who inhale it the ability to see what is invisible until the dawn. Remember?' He leans down and closes his eyes and sniffs. It is a faint but beautiful scent: like almonds, ambergris, honeysuckle. 'You too,' he tells Elva. 'Come on.' He helps her down and Elva kneels in the snow and inhales.

'Oh wow, that does smell lovely.' And then she opens her eyes. 'Look, Roan, look! The hawthorn tree!' They look together and see that it is glowing now, with a pale green light, which shadows move across as though dancing in a ballroom.

'Somebody's underneath,' Elva says. 'Invisible people are there.'

XIX

Now, this is probably a good time to tell you something about faeries.

I'm assuming you've never seen one, in which case you probably spell it 'fairies' with an i. ('I for idiot', some faeries would say, but I think that's overly mean.) Perhaps you've got the idea that they are elf-sized so live in bluebells or toadstools; you imagine they glow with supernatural light like fireflies and carry miniscule wands. But real faeries are the same size as you or I.

The truth, then: although they can shapeshift, taking the form of deer, cats or hares, they usually look like humans. They are eternally young and can live for more than a thousand years. It can be hard to identify one, if they keep their wings – iridescent like a dragonfly's – tucked into their cloaks. One helpful clue is that faeries always have green eyes.

Faeries live underground, but often come out on moonlit nights to dance. The portals between Elfland and the human realm are doors in faerie trees, most frequently hawthorn or ash. Tell-tale marks of these balls are often left in faerie rings on the ground.

The balls themselves are notoriously rowdy, with harps that play themselves, violet cocktails in crystal glasses, and capers until dawn. There are anecdotes of careless faeries bringing young men and women to dance at the revels every night then wiping their memories in the morning, causing them to waste away from lack of rest. Faeries are not always good, you see. Those of the Unseelie Court are brutal thieves and best avoided, whilst even those of the Seelie Court, who are kind and helpful, are quite capable of mischief.

Beneath the hawthorn tree's scarlet fruit, the faeries Roan and Elva discover are of the Seelie Court. As they approach the tree they can see it is whirring with merriment and dance. Faeries are nibbling canapes of crickets piled on ice, and vol-au-vents filled with their favourite mushrooms: blewits, penny buns and scarlet elf cups. They gossip over damson wine, wearing tiaras of holly; curtsey in skirts woven from spiderwebs bright with dew; whirl round and round with joined hands.

Roan and Elva dismount their horses. As they get close to the edge of the faerie ring, Roan sees Elva striding forward, her toes hovering over the boundary of mushrooms.

'Stop, Elva,' Roan whispers. 'Wait. We should wait at the edge. Faerie rings are meant to be dangerous.'

'Like giants?'

'I think we should wait.'

'Fine.'

They wait. After a few moments a faerie abandons her conversation, glides towards them and smiles warmly. She has white-blonde hair in plaits and eyes the green of pond-sedge, shining with emotion. Beads of water glitter on her wings and dress, although she isn't shivering. 'Hello,' she says. 'I've been expecting you since I saw you at the lake. I am Vivien.'

'The Lady of the Lake!' Elva says. 'Oh wow, what an honour to meet you!'

Vivien gives her a hug, almost too hard. 'No, it's an honour to meet *you*, Elva, you wonderful girl.' She shakes Roan's hand. 'And you too, Roan. You are a brave pair. Your hand is cold though, Roan. Here.' And she takes a burning torch and lights some logs by their feet with a whoosh. Elva and Roan thaw their numb fingers by the toasty fire.

'I'm sorry I can't invite you into the faerie ring to join our Samhain ball,' she continues. 'It's just that time works a little differently for faerie folk. You were right to hesitate, Roan. You might step in here for one dance, and when you step out ten human years will have passed. I don't think that would be very useful for your quest. Once a man accidentally fell asleep in a faerie ring and when he awoke his children were older than he was.'

'Why are you here in Carbonek?' Elva asks. 'We thought no one was left. I mean, you've travelled so

98

far, like we have… The flower said we should come here and speak to you.'

'Please sit,' Vivien says. She steps outside the ring to join them, and gestures to a fallen log where they all sit down. 'Mushroom canapé?' she offers, holding out a platter. 'These ones are puffball. It's true, you know: faeries do love mushrooms. Or a nice crunchy grasshopper, perhaps?'

Roan takes a mushroom nibble. 'Erm, thanks.'

'We faeries always have a party here at Samhain,' she says. 'It's the liminal time, when the portals open. I thought of not coming – it didn't seem appropriate somehow, to party amongst such devastation – but then I realised you two would be here. I've been following your adventures. All the magic folk have. And I wanted to tell you what I know, in case it helps.'

Vivien begins to tell how, when she was young and foolish, she fell in love with a wizard called Merlin. Handsome then, with a sweet soft face, he had slightly distant eyes that made him seem mysterious and deep. They were inseparable. But over time they began to grow apart.

Vivien started to realise that Merlin had very little real magic power, and the things he could do were cheap, sleight-of-hand tricks which only entertained the court. He also became increasingly bitter and angry at women who could do actual magic: Arthur's half-sister, Morgan le Fay, and Vivien herself. He decided it was wrong of Vivien not to share all her magic with him, when he was the king's wizard and therefore the most important in the country. He forced her to take him through her every spell, step by step, then got furious when he couldn't make them work. One day he slapped her face and called her a nasty little witch.

'What a liar he is,' Elva says, indignantly. 'In Camelot, Merlin told everyone that *you* wanted *him* to teach *you* all *his* magic! It was the other way round!'

'Yes,' Vivien says. 'And he also told people I was getting too powerful and plotting to turn his spells against him, so he ended our relationship. In truth, that was the other way round too. It was me who told him it was over.'

'How did he take it?' Elva asks.

'Not well,' Vivien says. 'It was then that Merlin came here.'

'Here?' Roan gasps. 'You mean he's behind this wasteland?'

'I think so,' Vivien says. 'At least, I'm fairly sure of it. The story goes, he was too heartbroken to stay in Camelot so fled to Castle Carbonek. But then everything here started to go wrong. King Pelles gave him the cave beneath his castle to stay and practise magic in. A spring flows through it, feeding into

the river. I'm sure he's poisoned it. And this poison has seeped into everything – it's not only killing the plants and animals, it's killing magic. It's draining the land of magic.'

Vivien points at the shadowy oak. 'Do you see the oak over there?

'We passed it,' Roan says. 'It looks so ill.'

'It's the oldest tree on this island. The oak of oaks. Every winter solstice, a ceremony is held here on the shortest day. Magic folk gather around the oak and cut down the mistletoe; we must catch it and make sure not a single white berry hits the ground. And then at dawn the wren, who is the Winter King, and the robin must fight, and the robin must win. Sorry,' Vivien mutters to the little wren they suddenly notice is perched on her shoulder, dumpy and buff like small child's shoe. 'That's the way it is, your Majesty.'

The wren twitters angrily and loudly. 'I know you could win if you wanted to,' Vivien says sharply, 'but that's really not the point.'

'Anyway,' she continues, 'after this ritual the sun's ebbing is reversed, and the year is reborn. New magic can begin.'

'But there was no mistletoe on it when we passed,' Roan says.

'No,' Vivien replies. 'The mistletoe is dead. And last year there was no robin. We think one of the starving families might have caught him in a net to eat. The poisoned waters were already taking their toll, but after the solstice the year got stuck and things have rapidly tipped from bad to worse. Newness is essential for magic: without it nothing can be transformed. Some faeries who shapeshifted before the winter solstice got stuck in their shapes. I'm afraid. If we can't heal the land and break this deadlock, the darkness might spread further. It's a contagion. Even as far away as Camelot I've felt my own powers ebbing, and there's a taint in the water.'

'My mum,' Roan says, in a weird voice, choking on his emotions. 'It's made my mum sick.'

'Yes, we're all connected to each other. Only some are showing it now, but we'll all sicken soon. All of Britain might become be a wasteland.'

'So, in that case, what about this cup?' Elva asks, coolly determined to get as much information from this faerie as possible.

'I don't know,' Vivien says, quietly. 'I hope it exists, for everyone's sake. It is said the grail can heal, by whatever magic, and perhaps it could heal the land. But if it is at King Pelles' castle, surely Merlin would have it already, or Pelles would have used it to save his kingdom? There is only one rumour about the grail that might explain this: it can only be seen by those with pure hearts.'

'Is King Pelles still in his castle?' Roan asks.

'Yes,' Vivien says. 'Wounded and alone – all his servants and knights have abandoned him now. Since the… well, you'll see. You must go to him in the morning. If the cup exists it could save the whole land. We can't let it be another trophy for the knights of the round table. Now come – let us make you a camp. We can promise great comfort until dawn, although I'm afraid it might end quite abruptly.'

'Thank you,' Roan says, relieved he doesn't need to build one himself in the dark. 'That would be great.'

'I will say goodbye for now,' Vivien tells them, 'as we faeries will be invisible again by the time you awaken. But before that, let me give you a gift that might help.' With this, she hands Elva a gold chalice set with enormous, twinkly rubies, emeralds and diamonds.

Elva's eyes go wide, the flames shining in them: surely this isn't the Holy Grail? Could it be? But even if it's not, with such riches she and Roan could be free forever! 'WOW!' she says. 'What is this? It's so—'

'Wait before you thank me,' Vivien replies quickly. 'I'm sorry to say it's not the Holy Grail, and it's not even real gold. It's just a chalice made of faerie gold.'

'Oh,' Elva says. 'I've heard of faerie gold. You mean it's fake. It's just a trick?'

'Yes. You've no doubt heard tales of faeries fooling people, bribing them with golden jewellery that is really made of old rags and slug-snot? This is another of those illusions. Within the week this chalice will turn back to gorse and pebbles, if my weakened magic even holds that long. But,' Vivien adds, 'there is, well – let's just say a rather greedy dragon has nested near the castle, and it never hurts to have a bribe on you for safety's sake.'

XX

It is not at all pleasant to fall asleep on a soft silken cushion under a thick blanket and wake up flat on your back in the mud with a pillow of compacted snow, a cold wind howling all around you. If you don't believe me, try it.

'UGH!' Roan shouts, startling awake. 'What? Yuk! AGGHH!'

'Huh?' Elva says, jolting upright. 'Why's my bottom damp? The tent! Where's the tent?'

But it is dawn, and the faeries have disappeared. Disorientated in the pink light, Roan and Elva scramble to their feet. They bolt breakfast. There's no tree to wee behind without stepping into the faerie ring, so they each turn their back whilst the other empties their bladder. There's no clear water to splash their faces. No point hanging around now, with the end of their quest within sight.

Mounting their horses, they ride towards the castle, which this time does not recede. There is a kind of wet sleet falling, which is worse than the snow was for making their joints ache. The snow on the ground is turning into that horrible, half-melted beige slush.

'So we just need to get into that castle,' Elva shivers. 'But Vivien said there was a dragon.'

'Look,' Roan says, pointing at a vast, slimy pellet of poo with a bone jutting out of it. 'Dragon dung.'

'Oh, delightful.'

'And footprints.' The big five-toed prints and tail drags seem to be going the same way as them, towards the dark, jagged castle. As they get closer, they see Castle Carbonek is perched on a large black rock, with carved stone steps winding up towards the castle gate. At the base of the rock is a large cavern, from which a rivulet of belching, dark green water pours down towards the river.

'The dragon has nested in there,' Roan says. 'I bet it's a withertooth. Large and black with blood-coloured eyes. There's a head of one in the Great Hall. They're meant to be weak, lazy fliers, but produce the hottest flames of any dragon. Oh, and withertooths gather shiny things, a bit like magpies. They nest in the bleakest abandoned places they can find because they only need to eat once a year, and their overriding instinct is to guard treasure. A wasteland like this would be perfect.'

'You sound almost excited,' Elva says dryly. 'Thanks for the factcheck.'

'I've never seen a large dragon that's alive before,' Roan mumbles, apologetically.

'Your lucky day, I guess.'

They edge nearer to the cave and suddenly the horses rear and neigh with fear. 'It's okay, it's okay, calm, calm,' Roan tells Valiant. 'I won't make you go closer if you don't want to. Here,' he jumps off, and helps Elva down from Goldentrot. She gets her crutches and the gold chalice from the saddlebag.

The ground is slippery. The toxic spring water has splashed and hardened to green glass with black bubbles caught in it. A strong, inhuman, chemical smell. Though they walk as quietly as they can towards the rocky steps, Elva is aware that her crutches sometimes land heavily. They are both absolutely shaky with adrenalin.

Another step, another. They are almost at the bottom of the stone steps and they can see something glinting in the cave. It looks like piles of coins, necklaces, cutlery, bracelets, bits of armour, some shiny stones. 'Treasure,' Elva says.

'ROOOOAAAAAAAR-RRRGHHHHH!'

At that word, the dragon's head, a real actual withertooth's head, lurches through the door of the cave and straight towards them. Fire hoses from its nostrils, charring the ground. Roan gives a very high yelp.

The beast pauses. Its arid crimson eyes stare unblinkingly at them, sizing them up. Its skin is black like oil is black, puddled with rainbows, stretched thin at the wings over fans of bone. Yellowed claws make a horrible scratching noise against the stone, *skreek skreek*. Then:

'ROOOAAAAAAAARR-RRGHHHHH!'

Another blast of fire. Roan covers his face instinctively.

It catches one of Elva's crutches and turns it into a torch. It must catch on her hair as well because there's that fried egg-smell. 'UGH, you stupid STAMPCRAB!' Elva yells, waving the burning crutch in front of her, her face crumpling with frustration. 'Ugh! That's my crutch, you harecopped horrible NEWT!' She hurls it onto the slush and rolls it round to douse it, and slaps wet fistfuls on her hair and clothes as well.

Roan watches the dragon as it watches her. He can see it is a moment away from attacking. Her neck looks so vulnerable suddenly, as she bends over the crutch: the pulse in it. 'Elva,' Roan says, as calmly as he can through the fear. 'Remember what you said when we started. *We're* the monsters.'

'You WHAT?' Elva demands, as behind her the dragon opens its jaw to show it puffy gums and its two rows of sharp, stale teeth. 'I didn't mean compared to THIS!'

'All it knows of humans is we slaughter dragons and steal their treasure, right?' Roan says.

'Right,' Elva says, trying to trust him.

'So how does it know we're different?' Roan asks. 'We have to show it.' Suddenly, he stands between Elva and the dragon and does a clumsy little bow. 'Erm, dragon, hello. I'm Roan. Please. I don't know if you can understand me, but – we don't want your things. I promise you: we don't want your things.'

The dragon tilts its head slightly. It growls.

'We just wanted to visit the castle, you see?' Roan says. 'We won't disturb you any longer.'

The dragon blinks those blood-irised eyes. Its eyelids seem so heavy, as though it can hardly lift them.

'It's tired,' Roan says, realising something. 'Elva, look, did you see that? It's tired. Its eyes aren't blood-coloured. They're bloodshot! It's exhausted. It's exhausted from always protecting its treasure. It must be so lonely, just standing guard twenty-four hours a day, never being able to rest.'

The dragon blinks heavily again. 'You need to sleep.' Roan tells him. The dragon looks at Roan and slowly, slowly nods. It makes a sound almost like mewling.

Roan gulps. Carefully, he sits down next to the dragon then softly pats the floor. 'Rest your head. You can trust me. We'll keep lookout for a while if you like.'

And it works! The dragon almost seems to sigh with relief, then suddenly flops heavily to the floor, its huge black head landing like a horned cannonball on Roan's lap. It begins to snore, tiny flames igniting round the edges of its nostrils on each out-breath. 'Oh,' Roan says, trying to move his shirt out of the way of danger. 'Erm.'

Elva is smiling. 'You really do have a way with animals,' she laughs. 'A withertooth. An actual real withertooth sleeping on your knee, Roan!' And he smiles, and strokes the tiny warm scales of its skin.

'It's kind of cute, actually.'

'Don't push it,' Elva says.

XXI

Did you forget the knights of the round table?

Roan and Elva might have done, but this is a grave mistake. If they were to look back across the endless poisoned fields this minute, they would see the knights are very close.

The rogue knight Tarquin did indeed provide as much distraction as could possibly have been hoped for – Sir Lancelot, Sir Galahad and Sir Lionel each had a go at fighting him, whilst Sir Bors got so bored waiting for his turn that when he saw a juicy boar going in the opposite direction he decided to pursue that instead.

Finally, after fighting until dawn, Sir Lionel beat an exhausted Tarquin just as Bors was getting back from a nice breakfast. Sir Lionel's fury was quite a thing to behold – his flaxen hair at manic angles, sour eyes, his big jaw chuntering with rage. 'You abandoned *me* for a bacon sandwich?' he roared. 'Trying to get in on my boar-ballad glory whilst I was fighting my socks off, were you? What kind of brother does that?'

And then he leapt on Bors, putting a knife to his throat, and the other two knights had to prise him off.

'LET ME AT HIM!!! I'll get you, you disloyal dew-beater! Aut neca aut necare!' he continued to splutter. 'That means kill or be killed in Latin, you dolt. All my life I've had to drag around my stupid brother, but you're no longer my family! I'LL SLAUGHTER YOU!'

Now, if your brother said those things to you, you might cry or at least feel a little bit bad, but since he was a tiny baby Sir Bors had only ever felt one emotion, which I suppose we might call 'red'. He grabbed his weapons and got stuck in. The fight lasted further hours, with Tarquin watching in bafflement before fate intervened and Sir Lionel was finally immobilised by a cramp.

After the brothers reached a truce, there was, of course, nothing left to distract them at the Castle of Maidens. Their official map led them smoothly through the wasteland, and now it's now.

So, where were we? Oh yes – Roan has got over the isn't-this-exciting-there's-a-dragon-on-my-knee stage, and is now in the how-on-earth-can-I-get-this-dragon-off-my-knee stage.

'Come on,' Elva whispers. 'Just slip out.'

'Just. Slip. Out. Thanks for all your help, Elva.'

'I didn't tell you to rock the withertooth and sing it lullabies, did I? Just slip out quietly. Nice smooth movement, got it?'

Roan softly, softly tries to inch out and then—

'ATTACK!' yells Bors, and – *twang, whheeee, thunk, thunk, thunk* – an arrow hits the stone just inches from Roan's foot. He ducks as another skims his hair. 'KILL THAT DRAGON!' yells Bors, and Roan looks up to see the four knights aiming at the withertooth. *Twang, whheeee…*

Thunk. Oh no, they have hit it! Blood is actually pouring from a wound: an arrow is plunged deep into its back. The dragon rouses its huge head, still half-asleep, maddened by dreams and undreams

'ROOOOAAAAAAAR-RRRGHHHH!'

Roan manages to throw himself on the floor and rolls out of the way just as a spray of the fiercest, most knight-melting flames in existence blast from its mouth.

'Let's go,' Elva says, grabbing his hand and pulling him towards the steps. 'Quick, Roan, please.' But it's too late. Roan's already started to shout. He can't help himself:

'You HURT IT! It wasn't doing any harm – it was just sleeping, you MONSTERS!'

Regret is immediate.

Sir Lionel slides back the visor on his helmet and looks over Roan with utter contempt. His eyes skim across the dark hair, long lashes, full lips and dirty tan.

Dog boy waits tremulously for the moment of recognition.

Why did he draw attention to himself? *Why?* As soon as Sir Lionel realises it's him, he's done for. They'll throw him in the dungeon. Maybe he'll never see his mum and sister again. His mum will die and it will be his fault. Why did he speak back? He's a lubberwart. A mongrel. Doesn't he know his place? The word *mercy* is ready on his tongue; begging's familiar flavour. *Mercy, mercy.*

'What's it to you, you stupid little mumblecrust?' Sir Lionel says, lining another arrow up in his bow and looking back towards the dragon. 'Shoo back to your manky old master and count yourself lucky I have a beast to slay.'

Master! He said Master! It takes a moment to sink in. Sir Lionel thinks King Pelles is Roan's master! How is it possible that Sir Lionel could not recognise his own servant? Could see someone every day and never see them? But he has just completely looked through his own dog boy, and Sir Lionel's indifference to his staff is a crazy relief.

Roan glances at Elva and sees her surreptitiously chuck the golden chalice onto the dragon's glittering heap. It rolls in amongst the coins and jewellery. 'HEY KNIGHTS,' she yells. 'LOOK, THIS DRAGON HAS

THE GRAIL! LOOK ON ITS TREASURE PILE!'

Always fans of gold and jewels, the knights believe Elva's fib. They spot the faerie chalice and get excited. 'She's right,' Sir Lionel barks. 'That cup must be the Holy Grail! It's mine!'

'To clarify,' Sir Galahad interjects, 'it is prophesied that the purest most righteous brilliant greatest knight ever will win the grail!'

'No,' Sir Lancelot cries. 'Sir Lancelot shall win the grail to glorify his beloved lady!

> *Guinevere I aim to please*
> *Who is lovelier than cheese*
> *She deserves all the glittering prizes*
> *For having such sapphire blue eyeses.'*

'Lancelot,' Lionel says, 'that really is the most appalling poem.'

'STAB IT!' yawps Bors.

Twang, wheee…

Elva squeezes Roan's hand very tightly. 'Quick,' she says. 'Up the steps, Roan, while they're distracted. Come.' So it happens that the two children stumble up the black rock steps and enter the castle.

XXI

Castle Carbonek is empty and very cold. Roan and Elva pass through a huge entrance hall where everything is velvety with dust and a rat takes fright. It leads to another grand hall, where there must once have been feasting. A bowl of fruit is rotting on the table: plums furred like chicks, wrinkled apples, flies humming on pear-slurry. 'Hello?' Elva shouts. 'HEL-LO?' Only her echo replies.

Passing through a corridor, they disturb a number of bats. Puckered, pointy faces shriek as they slap through the air, making the children squat and hold up their elbows in defence.

Peering nervously into each room off the corridor, they eventually come across a great bedroom where the heavy curtains are all drawn. There is a faint outline of a body in the four-poster bed, as still as a carving on the lid of a tomb. 'Is he dead?' Roan whispers. 'What if King Pelles is dead?'

'I don't know,' Elva says. 'Come on, let's see.' They tiptoe forwards into the vile hush, through the smell of decaying flesh.

Two silken curtains draped at the sides of the bed are pockmarked by moths. A huge cobweb makes a third curtain, where an inch-long spider is eating a moth it has wrapped up like a gift for the king. And there is King Pelles. His crown is still on. He stares into space with glass eyes. Is he alive? So shrivelled is his skin, you can see the skull in his face. Elva shrieks, as she sees the tip of a worm dart out of the corner of his eye, then covers her mouth.

The skeleton's jaw is moving. 'Who are you?' says its voice.

'R-r-roan, your Majesty,' Roan stutters. 'I mean, I'm no one, but we came to help. We want to find the healing cup.'

'Did you know there's a worm in your eye?' Elva says. 'It's probably a maw-worm. They can live in your lungs. I think you need to see someone about it.'

'I am dying,' Pelles says. 'I will die soon, without the Holy Grail. But I deserve it. I deserve all this.' He gestures around the room with a bony wrist. 'I have brought doom to my own people. I am death's instrument.'

'Really?' Elva says. 'I'm sure you're not that bad.'

'Come closer,' the king whispers, in his rattling voice. 'Sit, sit. Perhaps you two are here to listen to my deathbed confession. I must tell the truth to someone. I need the truth to be set down. I need to tell you the tale of Merlin's visit.'

Elva and Roan find a couple of dusty stools and

pull them up. They have to try and dampen down their sense of urgency; to not keep checking the door behind them for knights (is that another roar they can hear outside?). But it seems right to sit and listen.

'As a young king,' Pelles begins, 'I had everything. I was born to rule a fertile land of plenty, known for its delicious apples and cheeses, its birds and butter-flies that could be seen nowhere else. I never had to lift a finger. As a boy I had every toy I wanted, even a toy castle populated by elves, who had to play with me every day. I was constantly told how wonderful I was, how generous, how brave, how wise, and indeed the world seemed to circle around me. There was only one shadow that fell on my life. Arthur. He was also a boy-king, and from an early age I heard rumours of Arthur's adventures. The legend of how Arthur got the crown, by pulling a sword from a stone. How Arthur drove back the Picts and the Irish; his battles with the Saxons in the west country. How Arthur's sword, Excalibur, was the mightiest sword; his wife the fairest in the land; his knights the bravest; his castle the most glamorous; his treasure the twinkliest; his wizard the most powerful. Arthur, people whispered, was the rightful king of Britain. *Arthur, Arthur, Arthur.* One day, when I was a little older and had children of my own, I caught my four-year old daughter playing: 'Oh knight of the round table,' she was saying, from the little wooden turret we'd had made for her, 'please save this poor princess from Carbonek! Take me to Camelot, the land of dreams!"

King Pelles' voice has become an almost inaudible rasp. 'A drink?' he whispers, gesturing to the window. He has left a flask on the sill to catch the melting sleet, lacking servants and being unable to move any further. Roan puts it to his drooping lips and he catches a drop or two on his discoloured tongue and continues.

'I had nightmares about Arthur,' he says. 'I couldn't enjoy my life. I feared him, but more, I was jealous of him. A seething envy that stalked my every thought. And then one day, his wizard showed up at my door. Merlin was younger then. He didn't have a beard, although he had an unconvincing pointy hat above his bland, shiny face. At first I was surprised – was this really the powerful wizard I had heard so many stories about? But then we had wine and talked through the night, and he is very charming when he wants to be. Persuasive. I fell, I suppose you could say, under his spell.

'Merlin told me he had come for a new start. He was heartbroken, and there were witches at Camelot who wanted to destroy him. Could he be my wizard instead? I was flattered, though surprised he would settle for Carbonek after the glories of Camelot, and said as much, but Merlin insisted that he preferred me to King Arthur and thought Carbonek had the potential to be even finer than Camelot was. He said he'd heard across the country of my generosity and intelligence, and had a proposal.

'Have you heard of Alchemy? It is the study of how to transmute one material into another. Merlin told me that, studying ancient spell books, he had stumbled on alchemy's secret, and would soon be able to turn anything he wanted into gold. 'Look, sire,' said, and he showed me a leaf that was indeed made of the purest gold. I realise now it must have been mocked up by a goldsmith, but at the time I was taken in, the detail was so exquisite. Merlin asked if he could use the cave beneath my castle for his experiments, and promised that greatness would follow. I would have a castle made of gold! I would be the wealthiest king who had ever existed, beating Arthur in that at least.

'For months he toiled down there. Every time I questioned why it was taking so long, he would show me a golden acorn or shell, some trifle, but enough to make gold-fever race through me again. I became consumed with greed. Toxic waste trickled from his cave. I could see it was getting in the stream, but he said that a small amount of pollution was a necessary evil. He kept demanding ingredients for his experiments – he needed jewels, corn, apples, horses, servants, coins... I sent them in there and they never came out.

'I first felt the chill of wrongness when a rosebush by the path turned entirely grey, even the flowers, like it was made out of stone. It made me think of a petrifying well I had been to as a child, where a witch had hung a dolly and a glove and made statues of them. It had scared me then and I was suddenly scared again now. But Merlin said it was a necessary step. 'If we can turn things to stone, gold is not far behind. It means my alchemical process is working. I can taste it, King Pelles. Can't you taste the wealth?'

'That autumn our crops failed, but still I let him continue. I felt we had gone too far to give up. He showed me a solid gold ear of corn. 'You see, it's working,' he said. 'Forget about this year's mangy grain. Your crops will soon all be like this. Then your castle too. Imagine. A golden castle, looking out on fields and fields of gold, and the trees heavy with golden apples, and gold around your queen's throat and every finger and you, robed in purest gold, the glory of Britain and the world...'

'It was lies, of course. Merlin was deliberately poisoning my land. I was a threat, you see, to Arthur, who won't be happy until Britain only has one king. But his armies were stretched, and so he sent Mer-

122

lin to destroy us. It was a kind of chemical warfare. Alchemical warfare. Everything blackened. Everything turned to ash. He made this living land a land of statues. My daughter became ill and my wife took her away. My knights sickened. My servants fled... One morning I looked from my balcony at the stinking river and bone-strewn marsh and saw a child so thin, so starving, it was picking woodlice from the underside of a rotten log and eating them, and only then did I realise what I'd done in my pursuit of gold. I could suddenly see clearly how many must have died. I fell to my knees and howled.

'Merlin laughed at me before he left, when I told him I felt ashamed and asked if he didn't feel so too. He said – I will never forget his words – he said: 'I hate what's wild as I hate what's magical. It's all untameable, subversive, uncontrollable. I hate anything that's not entirely within my power. But your land is in my power now, and so these black dead fields look beautiful to me."

XXII

As King Pelles' story finishes, Roan is crying. He's not sure why but he can't help himself. They are tears of frustration perhaps; tears of anger; tears of fear. Tears for his mother and sister. Tears for Elva. Tears for the refugees. Tears for the otters and the oak, the fish and the flowers, for every small suffering thing. He is crying and crying, and Elva is patting his back. 'There, there.'

'Thank you Roan,' King Pelles says. 'I cannot cry anymore, but someone should cry.'

Outside, the struggle for the chalice still continues. The battle-cries and reptilian moans; the odour of burning.

'What about the grail?' Elva says at last. 'Please, King Pelles. Does it exist, do you think? Is there any hope?'

'Long ago,' King Pelles says, 'a lifetime ago, before all this horror, another stranger stayed here. He was called Joseph, and he had sailed here from the east. He said to thank me for my hospitality, he had hidden a precious cup in this castle which the world might one day need. But there were rules, he said, to protect it from falling into the wrong hands. I realise now, he meant hands like Merlin's, for I would have given Merlin the cup gladly, if I'd had it. I remember telling Merlin of it and his eyes gleamed, but he could not solve the riddle any more than I could.'

'There's a riddle?'

'Yes. And Joseph said that it could only be solved by one with a pure heart. There have been many attempts. But perhaps, before I go into the unknown, there is time for one more.'

Elva swallows. Her back is pure pain. She's pushed it too hard, she's been too brave, and now she feels hollowed out, like she has nothing left, but she has to keep going. 'Can you remember the riddle?' she asks him.

The skeleton king trembles; he seizes his chest. For a moment he looks like he will die there and then, taking the riddle with him. But instead he licks his crisp lips and begins to recite, in a voice like dried grasses:

> *I am pale as a unicorn, dark as a crow,*
> *high as Heaven and low as a burrow,*
> *sweeter than plums, sharper than salt,*
> *mild as lambs and wild as the colt,*
> *I am heavy as crags and light as breeze,*
> *but even dearer than all these.'*

'It's a riddle,' Elva says. 'It's a riddle, Roan.'

Roan looks up at her through his wet lashes. He nods. He wipes his eyes and nose on his sleeve.

'Alright, Elva,' he sniffs. 'Let's solve it.'

'Let's be logical about it,' Elva says. 'How can something be pale and dark? Is it something pied like a wagtail? Maybe a bird that burrows, because there's that 'lower than a burrow' line. I've heard puffins do – they're black and white so that would work. I've never eaten one, although Merlin was saying they're delectable at that feast so maybe they're sweet. But they're not heavy as crags. Oh, cows are – they're black and white, aren't they? But then the last line doesn't really…'

But it's alright, it's really alright, because Roan knows the answer.

'It's nature speaking,' Roan says, softly. 'The answer is this world. It contains everything, doesn't it? The dark and the light, the salt and the sweet, the crags and the wind. Nature. It's nature.'

And the wooden grail is in his hands.

XXIII

King Pelles starts to speak, only it catches in his throat. He seizes his chest again and cries out; he is having a heart attack. 'Quick!' Elva says, and she splashes some water from the flask into the wooden cup and drips it into Pelles' mouth. The real grail is not at all like the golden chalice. It is simple, rough and unvarnished.

For a moment nothing happens; his eyes go still. 'Is he dead?' Roan asks, panic mounting. 'Is he breathing? IS HE BREATHING?'

Only then, something wonderful happens. The king blinks, and when his eyes open again they look younger. Colour starts to return to his cheeks, which seem to soften, as his breaths become stronger and steadier. The king flexes his fingers and rolls his neck. He shakes himself a little with surprise. He sits up. And the brown is returning to his hair and the flesh to his bones, and he spits out a worm onto the floor, and then King Pelles stands. 'How can I ever thank you,' he says. 'I don't deserve this. I don't deserve it.'

'Just thank us by deserving it,' Elva says. And she closes her eyes for a moment, to steady herself, and wishes so hard, and then takes a sip herself from the cup.

Elva waits.

There is a mirror in the room, a dusty full-length mirror in a gilt frame. After a minute she walks over to it, and pulls up the back of her dress so she can see her back in it: the sore hunched back, with her spine which is twisted like an S, like a serpent that wants to break loose. Nothing happens. Nothing changes. She looks at her uneven legs, her shoulder-blade, and nothing happens. The pain screws her tighter. Dizzy, she stumbles, and Roan catches her. 'Elva,' he says. 'Elva, Elva, are you okay?'

'Nothing's happening,' she says, in a broken voice. 'Why's it not happening, Roan? It's not fair. King Pelles is healed – why am I not healed?'

'I don't know,' he says, unable to understand. 'Maybe it's taking longer with you. Maybe we'll try again later. I don't know. You're a heroine, though, do you hear me? We got the grail. You're my heroine. Now we just have to get past the knights of the round table and a furious dragon and we'll be sorted.'

'Alright, Roan,' she says. She smiles at him through the sadness, and he smiles back. 'For you, I'll try.'

Roan puts the grail in his pocket and they pick up what's left of Elva's crutches and make their way out of the castle, down the stairs. Outside, on the wasteland, the fearsome black dragon has flung Sir Lancelot over to where the hawthorn is, and is now chasing Sir Bors and Sir Lionel that way too. They are on foot: Sir Bors' bum looks roasted, and Sir Lionel's spear-tip has been melted blunt.

Sir Galahad has slipped away from him, though, and is now grabbing the jewel-studded chalice from the cavern.

'GOT IT! YES!' Galahad declares, thinking he has won the grail, unaware the true one is knocking against Roan's thigh. 'Excuse me, everyone, I have completed the quest!' he crows, slicking back his hair with pride. 'Sir Lionel! Lancelot! I don't know if you've noticed, but I believe this formally confirms that I am the purest most righteous brilliant greatest knight ever and worthy of the Perilous Seat. Ahem, could someone listen to me, please?' He heads towards the others, holding his prize aloft, irritated they are so preoccupied. 'BEHOLD, EVERYONE! GALAHAD IS VICTORIOUS!'

In a flash, Elva has a plan. 'Help me mount Goldentrot, Roan,' she says. 'Quick.' He helps her up then leaps onto Valiant. 'Get that faerie chalice,' she instructs him. 'As fast as you can.'

Roan gallops up behind Galahad, nearer, nearer and – yes! He snatches the golden chalice from Sir Galahad's fingers. Roan and Elva thunder towards the hawthorn. They get closer to the other knights. Sir Lancelot sees Roan has the chalice and lunges at him with his sword. Roan thinks it cuts him. There's too much adrenalin to feel anything, but he sees blood bloom on the fabric over his thigh.

'Stop in the name of the fair Lady Guinevere!' Lancelot declares, as though she gives two hoots. Roan feels an arrow whistle past him. He can hear hooves – Galahad has mounted his steed now... is catching up.

'TO ME,' Elva yells, 'TO ME, ROAN, TO ME' and in a blur Roan throws the faerie chalice towards her. No, *NO*. It misses by inches and falls to the ground. Desperate, Elva braces herself and hurls her body from her horse with a horrible thud, and somehow crawls through the muck and grabs the chalice. Sir Lionel is approaching her, puffed up with humiliated privilege. 'Canis canem edit,' he spits, lifting up his spear to pierce her through. 'Dog eats dog, I'm afraid, child.'

But wait, because with her last strength Elva lifts the chalice and flings it as hard as she can in the direction of the faerie ring. It lands with a clang in the centre, at the foot of the tree. 'MINE!' Sir Lionel roars, turning and running towards the mushroom circle, as Lancelot, Bors and Galahad all pile in after him to grab their bejewelled prize and—

Elva has done it.

In an instant, the four knights seem to freeze.

Or not quite freeze: they start moving in very very ssssssssssllllllllllllloooooooooooooooooooooowwww mmmmmoooooooottttttttttiiiiiiiiiiiiooooooonnnnnnnn. (That says slow motion, in slow motion.)

When humans enter a faerie ring, you see, time behaves very strangely.

What will seem to them just a few moments later, the knights will step out of it clutching a fistful of gorse and pebbles, and find it is the middle of the night.

XXIV

'Are you okay?' Roan asks, running over to Elva.

'Are *you* okay?' Elva asks, squinting up at him. The sun is behind him, but she can see the blood blackening his leg. He pulls her up and they hug each other tightly.

'I'm okay if you're okay,' Roan tells her.

'Then we're okay,' Elva says.

'That was genius. How did you think of using the faerie ring?'

'The lesser-scented ghostbell told us, didn't it?' Elva shrugs. She looks at the weird, barely-moving figures of the knights. 'Hopefully they'll lose a few hours in there at least. So. I guess we need to head back to Camelot and do this whole entire journey again?'

'Not yet,' Roan replies. 'It wouldn't be fair not to help first. There's some healing that we need to do. Hey dragon!' he shouts over as the beast moans. 'Give us a minute – we're going to help!'

They soon locate the source of the poisoned spring in the cavern behind a treasure chest. Elva pushes the wooden grail under its gush, and they watch the water purify itself. They splash the pure water over the mouth of the spring, then all the water begins to come out glittering clear. Trickling into the river, you can see water cleaning water – how quickly the brightness flows downstream.

A thirsty slurp and Roan's thigh heals instantly; Elva's bruises and fractures from throwing herself off the horse are mended. Roan lets the dragon lap from the grail with its huge tongue and watches its wounds seal and vanish, its energy returning. Its eyes are not, after all, blood-coloured, but reveal themselves as brown.

They pour some on a stone holly-bush, which it greens itself as a hundred bright red berries burst up. 'I know, I'll pour some on the tree, the oak of oaks,' Roan says, and as he pours the tree does the most amazing thing: it begins to bud, then dangling cat-kins appear like lamb's tails, and then it thickens with verdant, wobbly-edged leaves, and then the acorns form in their little hats and drop whilst the leaves turn the colours of apricot and dandelion and clay and twindle to the floor, and the tree is back in season again, but healthy this time, the rot all gone. 'It's not stuck anymore!' Roan cries. 'We've unstuck it!' And with this, magic returns. An elf opens a door in the tree and pokes its head out.

'Well thank goodness for that,' it squeaks.

Then a branch dips suddenly, and bounces. 'Look, Elva,' Roan says. 'Look, the crow's landed there. That

crow that's been watching me.' And the crow flaps down to the ground, croaks and then also transforms. Roan blinks and it has become a faerie in a black dress, with wings like black lace, black hair, a narrow face and attentive fern-green eyes. The faerie gives a gasp of delight and wriggles her fingers and bare toes.

'Hurray!' she says. 'Oh, what a relief. And not watching *you*, by the way, Roan,' she adds, gently. 'Although I've enjoyed getting to know you. I was watching Elva.'

'Who are you?' Elva asks.

'I am the enchantress Morgan le Fay,' the faerie tells them. 'I was in the guise of crow last year when the solstice failed and I got stuck. I must thank you two for rescuing me. All magic folk have a great debt to you both for your kindness.'

'Not really, though,' Elva says, dipping her head and suddenly looking deflated. 'Not really. I mean, deep down we don't deserve any thanks. Roan just wants to help his mum, and I was just helping myself. I was just thinking of me. Only it didn't work, did it? The grail didn't heal my back after all.'

'Oh darling,' Morgan says. 'You can't heal what isn't damaged.'

'But—' Elva yelps, struggling hard to hold it all together, her eyes simmering with tears.

'Here,' Morgan le Fay says. 'They just got stuck too. Let me.' She walks over to Elva and tears a strip of fabric from her back in a swift movement, then traces her finger down Elva's twisted spine, as though undoing a complex zip, and they burst out – wings. Crooked, beautiful wings.

'Giving you away was the hardest thing I ever did in my life,' Morgan le Fay says. 'But I was told it was your destiny. I hope you can forgive me. Oh I'm so very very proud of you, my changeling daughter.'

XXV

So it is that Elva and Roan return to Camelot not by horse, but by sky. Goldentrot and Valiant stay at Carbonek, where King Pelles promises to take good care of them, and of all creatures from now on, in order to deserve his second chance at life. And Elva and Roan fly back home as part of an army of faeries, determined to storm the dungeons of Camelot before the knights return, and set the prisoners free.

Obviously, Roan can't technically fly, but the magic folk provide him with a ride by griffin. An actual real griffin, with a muscular, deep-chested lion's body and an eagle's hooked beak and vast wings. Clutching tightly to its furred sides, Roan soars above Carbonek, where he can see green spreading out across the black fields as they heal. He flies through the clouds and over the mountains and rainforest, giants and fauns, the herds of unicorn and deer.

And Elva – oh Elva soars and dips and flutters and wobbles and dives! Reddish and dappled, her lopsided wings are the colour of a high brown fritillary butterfly's, suiting her perfectly. And the feeling is overwhelming: Elva feels like herself.

It takes only an afternoon, by this quicker route. The faeries can be invisible if they want, of course, but Roan on his griffin is not, so they land at his favourite spot in the woods, a little distance from the castle and its gates. 'I'll stay with the faeries,' Elva says to him. 'Here,' and she hands him the grail to tuck under his tunic. 'Good luck with your mum.'

Roan who has barely thought about his mum for hours, feels clammy suddenly with fear. Maybe it's unlucky he hasn't thought about her. Maybe she's died whilst he wasn't thinking about her. Maybe she's dead and it's his fault. Maybe he's too late. And his sister – what's happened to his sister?

'*Go*,' Elva tells him. 'The quest is over. Go to them quickly, Roan. Go.'

Roan runs to the drawbridge, getting out of breath. The watchman is chatting to John the groom. 'Hey, it's the dog boy,' the watchman barks. 'Dog boy, where've you been? You're in big trouble, lad. John here's had to sleep with the dogs. Everyone thought a wolf must've got you. Wouldn't be surprised if they throw you in the dungeon for playing truant like that. Well? Cat got your tongue?' Roan starts coughing. He's shaking again. The grail rattles against his chest.

John the groom looks Roan up and down kindly. 'Give him a break, mate,' he tells the watchman. 'His mum's really ill. She told me Roan was looking for herbs for her. She's, she's really on her last legs, poor thing. Not sure she's opened her eyes the last few days. Everyone loves Bonnie, don't they?'

'Aye, they do,' the watchman agrees, grudgingly. 'Give my love to your mum, son.' He ushers Roan past.

Mum is unconscious. It's too late, he thinks. *I'm too late!* Roan runs towards his mother's room, clumsy, wheezy. He stops at the well on the way, to tip a juddering splash of water into the grail. He can hear all the dogs joyfully yapping and jumping in the kennel, as though they can smell their old pal, but there's no time to say hello. *No time, no time.*

Just round the corner now. He smells that homely

138

smell of bodies and sheets, but mixed in with something gross and metallic. Pushing open the door very carefully, Roan is queasily unsure what he'll disturb. Gwen, back turned to him, her hair extremely unbrushed, is patting a wet scrap of fabric onto her mum's sweating, unconscious yellow face and telling her a story.

'... And so the unicorn said 'Yippee, I love eating rainbow biscuit, yum!' The end. And now a very nice goodnight song that you like,' and then Gwen's trying to sing a lullaby their mother used to always sing to them:

> *Lullay, mine liking, my dear child, my sweeting,*
> *Lullay, my dear heart, mine own dear darling.'*

Except she doesn't sing 'dear darling' – she's misheard it and sings 'near far thing' and it's very out of tune.

'Gwen,' Roan croaks softly, his voice clenched. 'Hey, sis.'

'ROAN!!!' Gwen shouts, leaping up to see him and exploding with excitement. 'YES!!!' She bounces up and down, waving little victorious fists in the air and almost spilling the water. 'I have been really really brave and helpful. Can I tell you my biggest number? It's seven hundred and fifty eight, and Muma says you will play with me for being so good. Will you play?'

'Just wait a minute,' he pleads. His sister is unbelievable. Then he looks at his sleeping mother. 'This first, this first, I need to give this to Mum first.' Dizzy with anxiety, he prises Bonnie's comatose mouth open a little. A blister on her bottom lip. Breath hissing through the space left by her missing tooth.

His mother's lovely face. *Please, please.*

And Roan pours a drop onto her tongue, a luminous bead, *drip*, and then another, another, *drip, drop, drip.*

Sometimes miracles happen. Not always, it's true. But sometimes good beats evil. Sometimes lost things are found; the blossom comes back. Sometimes we're saved.

Bonnie is saved by her son. In a moment, pink comes back to her cheeks and the pain goes. In another she opens her eyes and sees her boy. She can't stop grinning and grinning because he's back and he's hers and she thought she'd lost him, and she hugs him too tightly and then Gwen wants a hug too and they all make a hug-pile on the bed.

'Tell me your day, Roan,' Gwen instructs him. 'Tell me your day.'

XXVI

This story is almost finished, but you will want to know, I suppose, how the court of Camelot comes to an end.

With his army and most trusted knights still away, and a number of guards busy chasing off the seven brothers from the Castle of Maidens (who had the nerve to try and 'rescue' Camelot's women), King Arthur is largely undefended. There are only a couple of minor knights remaining, with titles like 'The Tallest Knight', 'The Hairiest Knight' and 'The Knight who Can Eat the Most Sausages in Under One Minute'.

Also, King Arthur is in the bath when he hears the flurry of wings. Elva, Morgan and Vivien have arrived with their faeries to storm the castle. 'ATTACK THESE PAGAN LOSERS!' he yells through the narrow, slitty window, flailing for his bath robe.

When his few knights grab their weapons, though, something happens. The faeries fight back with a wonderful magic: they transform those weapons into wildflowers.

In one knight's hand, a longsword becomes a midsummer orchid; in another's a knife becomes a

141

rather floppy poppy. A pot of
boiling oil is tipped over and
a gentle, petal confetti tum-
bles down. A lance turns into
cow parsley. Someone tries to
stick a foxglove up the griffin's nose and he pecks it to
pieces. A club becomes a pretty
bunch of primroses and violets.
Another knight finds his arrows
are all corncockles. 'How can I
kill a faerie with a corncockle!!'
he shrieks, through the sneez-
es brought on by his hayfever.

'I've got only a stupid daf-
fodil!' his friend yells back at
him. 'HEELLLPP!'

Stripped of their murderous advantage, Arthur's
men run away screaming.

King Arthur, seeing this from his slit, seems unable
to know what to do, so he pulls on his armour awk-
wardly (it's always hard to get dressed when you're
wet, isn't it?) and hustles to his Great Hall, getting
hit by a couple of daisies and a stray buttercup on the
way. He sits down bullishly at his empty round table,
waiting for someone to give orders to. Where are his
flatterers? Where is his feast?

'Someone's going to pay for this!' he shouts to the trophies, but the slain dragon's heads say nothing. 'Service!' he shouts, banging the table, eyes nearly popping out with fury. 'I want SERVICE!'

Meanwhile, Elva remembers where the dungeon keys are kept – in the back of a kitchen cupboard. She flies towards that room where she spent so many miserable hours peeling turnips, and leans over a bubbling pot to grasp them.

'Elva, is that you?' comes a small voice, and she sees her it is Mum – her human mum – cowering under the table with a colander on her head for camouflage. 'What's on your back, child? Oh! It can't be!' And then there is a sharp gasp.

'Yeah, turns out I'm a faerie after all,' Elva mumbles, as coolly as she can, giving her wings a kind of shrug. 'I mean, it's not that big a deal. It's not that surprising when you think about – oh, you fainted. Never mind, I'll tell you later.'

After throwing a goblet of cold water on her mother, Elva remembers her urgent task and flaps down the stone corridors towards the dungeon. She is still learning that she has to beat one wing harder than the other to balance out her legs, so knocks a painting and a stuffed wyvern off the walls. When she reaches the narrow, twisting stair-case there isn't space to fly, forcing her to limp the last few steps, but at last she pushes her key into the lock.

It fits! YES! There is a beautiful click. Elva has freed the prisoners, like she promised!

The gates creak, then are flung open by a superhuman force and out they pour, starting to cheer: a river of goblins, enormous talking birds, catheads, werefoxes, trolls... even little Tom Thumb is there, hang-ing on to a troll's hat! All of them wild with relief, thanking and hugging and high-fiving Elva.

Meanwhile, Vivien finds Merlin. He is in the library, frantically flicking through dusty books, trying to find a spell to stop the faeries.

Merlin sees her soaked hem first. He looks upwards slowly, not wanting to reach that face that makes him feel so unmoored that he must call the feeling hate. 'Come now,' Vivien says to him, the disappointment in her eyes unendurable. 'I didn't think you'd be stooping to magic now.' Merlin's soft face sags beneath the long grey beard. His forehead is furrowed; there are bags under his eyes. She wonders how she ever loved this man.

'*Vivien,*' he spits. 'But how –?'

'Hush,' she says. 'It's over, Merlin. We know what you did in Carbonek. But power is a fragile thing. I always wonder why humans place such value on something so transient. I hope you enjoyed your moment of power. I hope it was worth it. Faeries, seize him!'

And so it is that Vivien leads Merlin to a jail inside a hawthorn tree, where as far as I know he still is now.

By dusk, King Arthur feels very alone. The whole of Camelot smells like perfume. 'KNIGHTS!' King Arthur screams again at his dimming round table, his voice becoming hoarse. 'SERVANTS! SUBJECTS! COME HERE OR I'LL PUNISH ALL OF YOU! MERLIN! MERLIN, YOU'D BETTER GET HERE WITH A SPELL RIGHT NOW! MERLIN, WHERE ARE YOU?'

His cries echo around the cold castle walls.

When a maid *does* finally scurry in with a candle she gasps, because King Arthur has accidentally sat in the Perilous Seat.

It is the beginning of the end of the age of Arthur.

XXVII

As the sun sets, Roan, Bonnie and Gwen climb up to the battlements and look around in disbelief. 'What the what?' Gwen yelps.

'Wow,' Roan exclaims.

'What have you done?' Bonnie smiles through the tears, putting her arm round Roan proudly and giving him a squeeze. 'Oh my marvellous boy!!'

Because this is the end of a real adventure, better even than in the books. The castle is fizzing with magic: giants see-saw on a catapult; pixies raid the kitchen; small dragons soar and snort sparks; werefoxes go through the bins; a gang of elves have tied up Pierce and Acwel and are jabbing them with gorse! The stables are open now – even the hayloft with the untameable creatures in it – and goblins gallop off on mares and unicorns. Vesper the peregrine falcon soars. Pocket the goat chews through a row of party dresses on a washing line.

'WHOO-HOO!' Gwen whoops, catching the carnival spirit and starting to pogo up and down. 'THIS IS BRILLIANT! THIS IS THE BESTEST DAY EVER, ROAN!'

And then Elva lands on the battlements beside them, in the rain of petals. 'Hi,' she says shyly to Bonnie and Gwen.

'Are you a FAERIE?' Gwen squeals. 'Oh. My. Gosh!'

'This is Elva, my best friend,' Roan tells his family, and they smile at each other. 'Wow,' he tells Elva. 'That really was an epic quest.'

'The lame changeling and the dog boy.'

'You were right about everything,' he says.

'Well, you did solve the riddles,' she admits. 'And you had a point about that crow.'

'I guess you'll be living in the wildwood now?' he asks.

'Only if you promise to visit,' Elva tells him.

'Try and stop me,' Roan grins.

'ME TOO!' Gwen cries out. 'ME ME! I WANT TO PLAY WITH FAERIES TOO!'

This is how it really happens. Or the way it looks to us, at least. And I have my own reasons, I confess, for telling this tale. Although Camelot ends, so many Camelots follow – so many brutal knights; such wars; such extinctions. I am the last faerie left in Britain. Faeries can live to be over a thousand, so I have hung on to my portal in this patch of ancient wildwood, but it is under threat now from those who would clear the land to build.

For some time I have lived on my memories, which seem to me as fresh as dew on a primrose. Before I go, I need to preserve how it was for those who did not write the history books. I am tired of people telling these tales and not mentioning the maids and dog boys and kitchen staff – or Roan and Elva, the real heroes.

Now listen: I know there is not much magic left, but the greatest forms still exist for you to use. They are called kindness and hope. Perhaps you've felt them. They can transform a life. They can make a moment worth living in.

Please, there's not much time. This world is like a faerie ring. It can feel you're here just a few fleeting days, then you discover your whole life has passed you by.

You must set off on your quest, child.

You must find your grail.

ACKNOWLEDGEMENTS

It is a dream come true to publish this book. Huge thanks to James and Emma at The Emma Press for all their work making it happen. Thanks also to Karl Knights for his brilliant advice, and to Reena Makwana for bringing this story to life with the most beautiful illustrations I could have hoped for. I would also like to thank Simon Armitage whose work has been a source of inspiration – it was after reading his translation of Sir Gawain and the Green Knight that the idea for this novel first occurred to me, whilst the concept of weapons turning into flowers was seeded by a similar sequence in his millennium poem 'Killing Time'.

As always, I would also like to thank my agent Jenny Hewson, my mum and my husband Richard. This book is dedicated to my children Gruff and Cate, who were my muses and first readers – I am so proud of you both and wish you many adventures.

ABOUT THE AUTHOR

Clare Pollard has published five collections of poetry with Bloodaxe, most recently *Incarnation,* and a pamphlet, *The Lives of the Female Poets*, published by Bad Betty Press. Her poem 'Pollen' was nominated for the Forward Prize for Best Single Poem 2022.

She has been involved in numerous translation projects, including translating *Ovid's Heroines*, which she toured as a one-woman show. Clare has also written a play, *The Weather*, that premiered at the Royal Court Theatre and a non-fiction title, *Fierce Bad Rabbits: The Tales Behind Children's Picture Books*.

Her debut adult novel *Delphi* was published in 2022. *The Untameables* is her first book for children.

clarepollard.wordpress.com
X @ poetclare
Instagram @ poetclare

ABOUT THE ILLUSTRATOR

Reena Makwana is a London-based illustrator who creates illustrations using drawings, embroidery and print. Her work is influenced by the city, characters, creatures, social past and present. She has produced work for clients including *Vittles, Pit Magazine, Endeavour Agency, Lecker, Big Family Press, OOMK* and *At The Table.*

reenamakwana.com
X @ReenaMakwana
Instagram @reena.makwana

ABOUT THE EMMA PRESS

small press, big dreams

☙❧

The Emma Press is an independent publishing house based in the Jewellery Quarter, Birmingham, UK. It was founded in 2012 by Emma Dai'an Wright and specialises in poetry, short fiction and children's books.

In 2020-23 The Emma Press received funding from Arts Council England's Elevate programme, developed to enhance the diversity of the arts and cultural sector by strengthening the resilience of diverse-led organisations.

The Emma Press is passionate about publishing literature which is welcoming and accessible.

Visit our website and find out more about our books here:

theemmapress.com
Facebook @theemmapress
X @theemmapress
Instagram @theemmapress